Never Say Nigger Again!

An antiracism guide for white liberals

M. Garlinda Burton

D1613552

James C. Winston *Publishing Company, Inc.*
Trade division of Winston-Derek Publishers Group

© 1995 by James C. Winston Publishing Company, Inc.
Trade Division of Winston-Derek Publishers Group, Inc.

First printing

Book and cover design by Alec Bartsch

Cartoon on page 42 by Doug Marlette
Cartoon on page 60 by Berkeley Breathed
All other cartoons by Kirk Anderson, Madison, Wisconsin

PUBLISHED BY JAMES C. WINSTON PUBLISHING COMPANY, INC.
Nashville, Tennessee 37205

Library of Congress Catalog Card No: 93-60415
ISBN: 1-55523-626-X

Printed in the United States of America

In humble tribute to Thurgood S. Marshall,
who never avoided confrontation in the
quest to change us all for the better.

Contents

Acknowledgements   vii

Introduction   1

White Liberals and White Racism   9

"Doing" Racism   17
Words and Deeds, Work and Play

PC: Politically Correct or Plain Courtesy   29
Why "Classical" Isn't; and, Never Say "Nigger" Again

The Trouble with Elvis and Larry Bird   43
When Imitation is *Not* the Sincerest Form of Flattery

How Black People Abet White Racism   51
Including the Politics of Hair Texture and Skin Color

What Your Black Friends   61
Won't Tell You About Your Racism

***Your* Rights as a Recovering Racist**   71

Making Your Home and Your Head   75
(And Your Children) Racism-Free

Bibliography   85

Acknowledgements

So many people make me who I am
and my thoughts what they are. I'm grateful to:

Larry Ingram, my once-in-a-millennium love, my husband;
"Muh," my mother, Margaret Burton, my most constant
    mediator and advocate;
"Roop," my brother, Rupert Burton, the world's best deejay,
    for extensive lessons on the politics of popular music;
Newtonia Coleman, who knows me better than just about
    anyone and stills believes I'm wonderful;
Two "rays" of sunshine, namely Ray Sells and Ray Waddle,
    who are credits to their gender and their race (smile).
    Thanks for surveying my book with open minds and
    honest eyes;
And Sally Voelkert, my oldest friend, my German-American
    cosmic twin, who always gets my point.

Introduction

This book is about white racism, but it doesn't take on the Klan, and it's not designed to redeem members of the White Aryan Resistance. It's not for conservative members of the Republican Party or John Birchers, if they're still around; nor is it for white people who make it a point to avoid any social encounters with black people.

This is a handbook, a question-and-answer book, a guidebook for white people who work with, live with, play with, and/or love at least one person who is African American.

This book is written for white people who think they don't need a book on racism. It's for former '60s activists, left-of-center Democrats, neighbors in racially mixed communities, parents, white public school teachers, environmentalists, white feminists, liberal Christians and Jews, partners in interracial marriages and other interracial relationships, and CEOs who have won awards for their companies' affirmative action policies. It's for all those white people who think they've got their racism licked.

Yes, white *liberals*—the ones African Americans live with, work with, and deal with on a daily basis. The majority of our encounters with racism happen with those individuals. Most African Americans have never had a one-to-one conversation with a Klansman, but most still suffer the pain of white racism on a regular basis—many times from white friends and colleagues who think they're simply *too enlightened* to harbor racial bias.

And while Klansmen, for instance, freely admit their racism, white liberal friends and colleagues often go to the mat denying theirs. Summarizing results of a reader survey on racism in the May–June 1992 issue of *Ms.* magazine, the writer concluded, "The *bottom* line? *Nearly one woman in three* [overwhelmingly White and ultra-liberal] *believes that she is not prejudiced at all*" (Malveaux, p. 26).

Or else, if they don't deny their racism, my white liberal pals often want a gold medal and ample praise for any strides they make in overcoming it. A white person who supports public schools and contributes to the NAACP is light years ahead of David Duke, right? Damned right. In a society such as ours, the fact that any white person ever swims against the tide of heritage, presumed entitlement, and peer pressure to enter into interracial friendships, to move into mixed neighborhoods, to advocate for equal rights, and to live in cities rather than suburbs is noteworthy.

But special praise and rewards? For what? For recognizing people as equals and treating them like human beings? For finally admitting that "American" historical records, traditional values, and language are tainted by cultural jingoism and lies? Is applause due those white people who acknowledge aloud that slavery was genocide, that Jim Crow was bogus, and that separate-and-unequal schools and housing are unconscionable? I'm sorry, but that's like giving a man the Nobel Peace Prize because he *doesn't* beat his wife. As progressive as my liberal friends may be on the subject of race relations, we've all got miles to go before any European Americans can truthfully declare themselves devoid of the taint of racism.

When it comes to white racism, it *is* possible to be both a pal and a part of the problem, and ally and an adversary. Combatting racism in the hearts of politically and socially progressive white people is, in fact, one of the last great obstacles to dismantling institutional racism at all levels in the United States. This guide is intended for every white person who has reached a point where she or he is ready to take the next step and tackle racism from the inside out. In the following chapters I outline what I see as some of the unique aspects of racist behavior as displayed by even the most well-meaning white liberals, explain how such behavior plays out in racially integrated environs, discuss personal and corporate racism commonly exhibited by well-meaning white people, and offer some first steps in helping progressive-thinking white people understand and root out their own racism.

As you read and explore the ideas discussed in the following chapters, you will likely feel pain, guilt, anger, indignation and frustration. I know, because researching and writing this book sometimes left me with similar feelings. We liberals so fervently wish that everyone could experience the United States of America as the undisputed "land of opportunity" and "land of the free," that when a horrific example of white racism makes national news, such as the 1992 acquittal of four white police officers for beating a black man in California, we are as wide-eyed, disappointed, and disbelieving as children during the 1909 Chicago White Sox scandal. Say it ain't so, Joe. Play that videotape again; the black guy must have done something wrong. This isn't the Old South of 1963—we don't "do" racism anymore.

But we do. And it's up to those of us who wear the liberal badge to stop pointing fingers at the South, while ignoring racism in the North; to cease merely talking politically correct lingo; to get off of our thirty-years-old, "voted-for-McGovern" smugness and complacency; and to take a radical new look at examples of white racism among those who thought they knew better.

Interestingly enough, as instances of white racism and racial separation have become less sensational (we seldom hear of mob lynchings and strange disappearances in the Deep South anymore), our willingness to talk honestly and strongly about racism has waned. We have forgotten the heated debates, public demonstrations, and painful legislative discourse responsible for the progress our nation has made. Many of the most ardent liberals no longer have a strong stomach for confronting white racism, since the battleground has moved from blocked voting booths to one's private domains, namely the neighborhoods, churches and synagogues, offices, social clubs—and inside our heads. But it is this too-close-for-comfort zone that we will visit in this book.

Advice From a White Liberal
on Facing White Liberal Racism

The Rev. Joseph Edward Agne, director of the racial justice unit of the National Council of Churches based in New York—himself a white liberal—says the only difference between a white liberal racist and a white conservative racist is that "one is liberal and the other is conservative."

In other words, Agne says, white liberals must recognize that racism is part of the White American condition, and that they themselves reap the benefits of and erect institutions bolstered by white racism. One who is truly committed to the fight against racism—as opposed to just waving a liberal banner and winning the NAACP "good white folk" award—must stand up and say, "My name is John (or Mary or Cynthia or Eddie) and I'm a white racist." At least say it to yourself.

To "do" antiracism, white people must make a conscious choice, an active choice—a choice to suffer some discomfort and sacrifice some power and some assumptions. For those white people ready to do antiracism:

Choose repentance over denial. "We have to quit denying that racism runs through us—and through us and through us," says Agne (p. 5). "Those of us who are White need to open ourselves to the experience that people of color have." Some white liberals deny that racism is anything other than isolated incidents incited by an ignorant few. Or they reject racism as a white power phenomenon, saying that black people and other people of color can be "just as bad" when it comes to racism. Much of this is a smoke screen—arguing semantics takes the heat off white people, and puts the blame on people of color.

But there is no denying that institutional power in the United States, indeed throughout the Western World, is white power. And power turns mere racial prejudice into a death penalty that is racially skewed, economic systems that deny health care to the poor, family values that deny non-European traditions, and political systems that afford the most clout to monied white men. Agne stresses that racism is a white issue.

Choose belief over doubt. When a black person says to a white person that something he or she experienced is racist, the "first response is often, 'Prove it,' and use white norms while you're at it," says Agne. "What would happen if we Whites would presume that if a person of color says something is racist, it's true until we are convinced otherwise?" Amoja Three Rivers advises, "If you do not understand or believe or agree with what someone is saying about their own oppression, do not automatically assume they are wrong or paranoid or oversensitive. Oppressed people survive by learning to trust their instincts. The well-meaning non-oppressed should follow our lead" (Three Rivers, p. 10).

Choose to address white people's racism, not just black people's powerlessness. George M. Daniels, a black pioneer in journalism in the United Methodist Church, observes, "One of the problems that I find with most seminars on racism is that Whites generally want to focus on Blackness—what's wrong with us, why we're not making it." An alternative, says Daniels, is for white people to admit that discussions with black people about racism frighten them. White people should talk about "why they are 'angry, frustrated, insecure, [and] guilty' about their racism"—why they're afraid to face racism (Daniels, p. 30). He advocates a subtle change from viewing racism as a problem for black people to seeing white racism as a chronic problem of white people.

"Working against racism on behalf of people of color has not worked [for white liberals or anyone else]," adds Agne. "We [Whites] need to understand that our own being is at stake."

Choose antiracism over nonracialism. Many people still insist that racism would go away if we'd all just stop talking about color, and just become Americans. But this color-blind attitude doesn't match social reality. Color blindness makes the serious error of assuming that racial differences are insignificant, claims educator Louise Derman-Sparks. The color-blind approach "has been a soothing view for whites, while blatantly ignoring the daily experience of people of color," she explains (Derman-Sparks, p. 6).

As Agne puts it, "The problem with the melting pot is that we [Whites] keep owning the pot." The issue is not erasing color; the issue is affirming and empowering people of color as equal partners at every level of governmental, social, political and economic life. Only then can our society deal honestly with racism.

Choose joining with people of color already doing antiracism. Again, white people who are sincere in their desire to tackle racism have to overcome their cultural bias against learning from other-than-white people, who are more qualified to lead discussions on racism. Survivors of white racism see more clearly its causes and effects, and white people who want to know about racism need to ask those experts.

Recalling the political activism of the 1960s, Agne notes that although white liberals worked for social change, "We formed a peace movement that was racist. We formed an environmental movement that was racist. Then we wanted to know why people of color wouldn't join our racist movement. . . . Those of us who are liberal seem only to feel comfortable as long as we are still in charge. We've got to deal with that—our racism and our need to control" (Agne, p. 6).

Commit to antiracism for the long haul. For too many liberals, the front-burner, politically correct agenda changes faster than hemlines. But white racism has been with us since Day One of U. S. history—it is a heritage. The fight against racism shares the same long history. One seminar at work, one move to an interracial neighborhood, or a once-a-year observance of Black History Month aren't going to end white racism. Those who are antiracist choose to be so as a lifestyle and a life-long avocation, and hand the baton to their children and grandchildren. Each generation has inherited our racism problem; how about passing along some solutions?

Author's Note

Although at least six broad racial groups (European American included) exist in the United States, this book deals primarily with the relationships between African Americans and European Americans in the United States of America, for three reasons:

- I'm African American and can speak with authority on the subject of being an African-American U. S. citizen confronting white racism in my native land;
- Although I acknowledge and respect the histories of all people of color and Jews in overcoming racism and anti-Semitism, I believe that racial polarization in the United States continues to be most severe between African Americans and European Americans. A prominent African-American minister and Civil Rights leader tells a story of how he had to don a turban and speak with a Persian accent while in a Dallas seminary in the 1960s in order to be admitted into the city's auditorium for a show. As a Middle Eastern student he was acceptable according to white society's rules; as a black man he couldn't get in the door.

  I've seen many old movies where beautiful Latina, Native American and Asian-American women are sought after by white men—even for the honorable institution of marriage—with little or no controversy over miscegenation. But where Asian-American actor Nancy Kwan could kiss William Holden on screen in the 1950s, African-American singer-actor Nancy Wilson dared not. And while I regularly meet white people who claim that their great-grandmother was a Cherokee princess, not many dare brag about their more likely black kin. You rarely hear a white person say, "My great-great-grandmother was black" or "One of my ancestors had a family with his black housekeeper, so we're thinking of inviting those cousins to our next family reunion."
- A majority of civil rights movements in the United States have borrowed the tactics, songs, organization, and rhetoric of the African-American movement, so strides in that area continue to lead the way for other liberation struggles.

UNNERVED BY THE BLATANT DISCRIMINATION AGAINST THEM, WHITE MALES BEGIN FORMING SUPPORT GROUPS, IN CORPORATE BOARDROOMS ACROSS THE COUNTRY.

White Liberals and White Racism

> "There is absolutely no way that you can talk about racism without doing two things right off: embarrassing black people and offending white people. There's no way to do it if you're going to tell the truth."
>
> *Neely Fuller, Jr., 1992*

When I got my first important newspaper job ten years ago, a white man and I were interviewed and hired within months of one another—him first. At company expense, the self-proclaimed editorially liberal newspaper brought each of us to the city to look for housing. The white man stayed at the home of the editor-in-chief and was squired around town to shop for houses by the managing editor, who had also contacted a realtor for him. During private dinners at colleagues' homes, he got informal but invaluable hints on how to succeed at the paper, learned about unwritten company benefits such as travel advances, frequent-flyer awards, and other perks, and was invited to join the prominent, downtown church that two of the staffers attended.

When they brought me to town—Black, twenty-three, and fresh from a small-town Iowa paper—I bunked in with the new white guy and his family in their still-unpacked new house. A young African-American intern, herself new to the city, was assigned to help me find housing. Although my salary (and, therefore, my housing options) was greater than hers, the intern was able to show me only what *she* knew and could afford, mostly in low-income areas, some of them inconveniently located and unsafe. She and I ate our lunches and dinners alone together, at our own expense (except for one lunch during business hours with the whole staff). No one told me anything about benefits, luggage and laundry reimbursements, or the special loan program at the credit union. I received only standard employee information through the company manual they shoved at me after I came on board....

. . . Recently, I found my friend Bill, a white television producer in his mid-forties, fuming because a dissatisfied client had mailed a letter of complaint to Bill's boss instead of sending it directly to Bill. Bill was furious because the client had gone "over his head." I told him about a file drawer in my office full of letters—countless letters of both complaint and commendation sent only to my white male boss, who was thoughtful enough to share "blind" copies with me. Bill was incredulous. In nearly fifteen years of work at our company, rare were the times a complaining client had gone overhead to his also white male boss. For me, it has been a fairly regular occurrence....

. . . While attending my first National Organization of Women meeting in Nashville, Tennessee, a smartly dressed, energetic white businesswoman approached me and plunged immediately into a conversation—no, a diatribe—about how she felt that white racism is "overdramatized" while sexism is underplayed.

"Nobody can tell me anything about discrimination," she said. "With the oppression I've faced and the opportunities I've been denied as a woman, I'd say I'm just as much a victim as any black man!"

Agitated, I had a ready reply. "Nobody ever lynched an upwardly mobile white woman for trying to vote," I said. "No one has ever murdered a white woman and tied a cotton gin around *her* neck for whistling at a fourteen-year-old black boy." After that I stopped calling myself a "feminist" and became a "womanist" (writer Alice Walker's coinage for women of color and others committed to eradicating all forms of oppression, uniting all of creation, and liberating people across lines of gender, class, race, sexual orientation, economic condition, or physical ability).

In *Portraits of White Racism,* author David T. Wellman debunks the existence of any "racism-free" white people—even liberals—in his chapter "Prejudiced People Aren't the Only Racists in America." Wellman's thesis is that, although college-trained, middle-income, left-of-center Whites—from whence spring a majority of liberals—learn the rhetoric of "tolerance" as part of their liberal education, it is erroneous to assume that they, therefore, are not racist in the way they actually live and interact with people of color. In fact, Wellman's research shows that, with the exception of southern white people, de facto racial tolerance "is not significantly related to social class or voting record." Without constant self-study, honest dialogue and interaction with people of color, and deliberate consciousness-raising, Wellman suggests that white people will follow racist patterns, no matter how liberal their stated or implied philosophies about justice and equality (Wellman, pp. 30–31).

I work for one of the most progressive and politically liberal non-profit organizations in the world: the United Methodist Church. Long before "political correctness" was in vogue, our nine-million-member, mostly white, global organization took public stands against oppressive child labor, domestic violence, and nuclear weapons. As a Christian denomination we have more women ordained as ministers than any other mainline Protestant church in the United States. We have one of the most racially diverse bodies in the world. We've boycotted South Africa because of apartheid, changed "mankind" to "humankind" in our hymns, continued to support eleven historically black colleges, and have started our first university on the African continent.

We are also chock-full of the nicest, friendliest, most sincere and progressive white liberal racists under the sun. Consider these recent comments made to me (or in my hearing) by my white colleagues:

- "I dressed up as our maid for Halloween this year. You know how black women dress, with their stockings rolled over their knees, their hair all over their heads and too much makeup? They are so cute!"
- "John [black supervisor] shouldn't hire Lila [black applicant] for the new manager's position. It won't look good to have three

Blacks on the management team. There are only four management positions altogether. People will be upset."

- "How can calling European music 'classical' be racist? That's the definition in the dictionary and the standard use of the word!"
- "Garlinda, I haven't seen you in a coon's age." (A really good friend said this one, so I pulled her aside privately and schooled her. She didn't know the history of the word "coon" as a racial slur against black people. She thanked me, and we're still friends).
- "I understand that you want the video crew to be racially mixed, but it's more important to have people who are qualified." (Can't we achieve both goals? Are only white people "qualified"?)
- "You wouldn't believe how prejudiced my Uncle Jake is, Garlinda. He called this man on the bus 'nigger' right to his face. Should I have said something to him?"
- "If Kala [a white receptionist turned down for a better job] had been Black, she would have gotten a promotion. With this affirmative action stuff, they'll only hire Blacks."
- "I'm not talking about you, but some Blacks are so destructive."

Not one of the above comments was made by a "bad" person. Friends and respected coworkers said these things. Not one of these people (well, maybe one) would consider herself or himself racist. They certainly don't mean to be. But racist behavior is in their bones, just as it is cloistered in the walls of churches, nailed into the beams of corporate America, tucked between the pages of academic texts, and written in invisible ink just above the bottom line of municipal, county, state, and federal budgets.

Individual acts of racism don't make you a bad person, and they certainly don't point to a person incapable of change. For all of us born and reared in this country, racial separation, mistrust, misunderstanding, and misinformation are legacies. *Most acts of everyday racism are unconscious, unintentional, and not malicious.* But just as the dog hit unintentionally by a truck driver is no less dead, people of color suffer the consequences of racism regardless of whether or not the offender *means* to hurt them. Until each can't-touch-me white liberal is willing to name her or his personal, conscious and unconscious acts of racism, claim them and wrestle them to the ground, no Civil Rights bill or Martin Luther King birthday celebration is going to mean a damned thing.

How can we make the needed changes? So many ways have been tried and have failed. We know what does not work. Affirmative action programs alone don't work, although they are necessary to ensure equal access. And I think we've learned by now that sending white people on guilt trips is out. With guilt trips white people become defensive and shut down, like a girlfriend who warned me recently, "You keep talking about racism, accusing people who are really trying not to be racist, and we'll just throw up our hands and say, 'I give up.'"

But I'm willing to risk losing some white liberal friends to that attitude, because while I'll agree guilt trips won't work, I believe some confrontation is pivotal. Not only must black people confront white people about their racism, but even more important, white people must take the next step and confront themselves and each other. Says Karla Braig, a Dubuque, Iowa, English professor and former chairwoman of that city's Human Rights Commission, "[Racism] isn't about Blacks, it's about Whites learning to live in a diverse society. We [Whites] have to settle this among ourselves" (McCormick and Smith, p. 70).

If you're reading this book, you're at least willing to consider helping to "settle this."

Try this self-examination. No one is keeping score, but use the following guide as a mirror to look at yourself and significant others in terms of possible unconscious participation in white racism. Do you ever:

- become uncomfortable, at least—and suspicious, at most— when you see several African-American co-workers lunching together or standing in the hall together talking? Have you ever jokingly accused them of "caucusing" or "plotting"?
- talk about how many black friends you have or your "really sweet" black housekeeper when you meet a new black person,

especially when the conversation turns to race or racism? Is that supposed to prove you haven't got a racist bone in your body?

- get defensive when a black person in your office criticizes the work environment you happen to like as "racist"? Is it tough to shake the feeling that accusations of racism are largely a result of black people's "over-sensitivity"?
- think it is possible for one who opposes marriage between black people and white people to still claim that he or she is not racist?
- praise black women with lighter skin or straight hair (like former Miss America Vanessa Williams or legendary beauty Lena Horne) as naturally more attractive than darker-skinned Blacks or those with Afros or dreadlocks (consider actor Whoopi Goldberg)? Do you assume that African Americans who speak without "an accent" (a matter of jingoistic opinion; *everyone* has an accent) are more intelligent?
- regularly describe predominantly African-American or Latino neighborhoods in your city as "bad" and "dangerous"? How do you know? Do you regularly visit friends or co-workers who live in these neighborhoods? Are there any white neighborhoods you describe as "bad"?
- double-check and scrutinize work by black employees and co-workers when you wouldn't think of doing so to white co-workers?
- allow a black employee under your supervision to be slack and lazy, or knowingly let her make a mistake on a report that causes her to fall on her face, all because you "don't want to seem racist"?
- buck your company's usual chain of communications and command when a black co-worker or supervisor is involved? Have you ever complained to the boss about a black co-worker before first approaching that co-worker directly and trying to work it out?
- constantly talk about "qualifications" when discussing affirmative action or hiring an African-American candidate, but not mention the word when talking about white applicants and coworkers? Do you assume that a white person who is hired or

interviewed for a job is qualified, but that African Americans are there mainly because of affirmative action policies?

- believe that affirmative action policies at your company go too far because there are "too many Blacks"?
- talk about Blacks you deem as qualified—maybe those having credentials, degrees, and goals similar to your own—as "outstanding," "exceptional," "articulate," as if an educated, articulate African American is the exception rather than the rule?
- think it's OK to quote racist remarks and slurs by other white people to illustrate someone else's racism? Is it *ever* appropriate to use the term "nigger"?
- let white friends and colleagues make racist remarks to your face without confronting them?
- celebrate Elvis Presley as the "king" of rock-n-roll, without giving a thought to African-American singers and performers who introduced the genre years before Elvis?

If you answered any of these questions in the affirmative, you have participated in some form of white racism. If you didn't answer yes, you may have trouble with denial, or you may know someone who needs your help to overcome their racism. In any case, please read on. Help is on the way.

"Doing" Racism
Words and Deeds, Work and Play

"Learning to believe they are superior because they are White, or male, or able-bodied, dehumanizes and distorts reality for growing children even while they may be receiving the benefits of institutional privilege."

Louise Derman-Sparks, 1989

As I encounter white racism among my colleagues and friends, the most common phrase I hear is, "I didn't think about that."

My oldest friend, Sally, my German-American cosmic twin, loves the book *Gone With the Wind*. I mean, she could read it every day. Once, when she was visiting me and reading it for the umpteenth time, she sighed and said, "Aren't there are times when you'd love to have a mammy?"

Few people in my life are as loving and wonderful as Sally, a public school counselor and deaf-education instructor who has a magic touch with children. We've been friends since eighth grade, when her parents refused to sign a petition to keep us—the first black family on the block—out of the neighborhood, and after we discovered a common love of Christmas and Mickey Mouse paraphernalia.

But "mammy" was something we couldn't share.

Sally never meant to hurt me. She just didn't think. We talked it through, and we both learned something, understood each other a little better, made our friendship a little more honest and real. To her, *Gone With the Wind* is Vivian Leigh being swept away by Clark Cable, the liberated woman fighting for her homeland and her way of life. For me, it's ebon-faced black women taking time from their own families to fret and fuss over a petulant white mistress. It's two African-American women turned into cartoons by a white writer and white filmmakers, the women participating in their own oppression and actually grieving with the white landowners when the Union Army comes to liberate them.

Think, I urged Sally. And she did, and we talked. I understood why *Gone* is her favorite, while she began to realize what the pre–Civil War South means to *me:* black people in bondage, families ripped apart, physical and sexual abuse an everyday occurrence. Hoop skirts, mint juleps and fiddle-dee-dee weren't our experience. And movies and books that portray pancake-flipping, would-die-for-Massa black servants are full of hooey, the folly of people who would deny the horrible flip side of plantation life. Says Amoja Three Rivers, "The loving, grinning, selfless, big-tiddied black mammy is part of the antebellum, Nigra Mythology that white folks have created to assuage their own guilt" (Three Rivers, p.11).

Why "Reverse Racism" Isn't

I was having lunch with one of the foremost white nonfiction writers in the United States. I was enjoying talking with him about his thirty-five-year coverage of the Civil Rights movement, including the Medgar Evers murder trials. It was a fascinating conversation, and my admiration for him and his politics swelled. He is a brilliant journalist.

The conversation naturally moved from the 1960s to contemporary issues of racism in media, and I looked forward to a conversation with an informed white man and journalistic colleague who didn't flub the discussion of race.

But no—when the talk turned to race relations, he started telling me about how it had really bugged him one day to walk into the newsroom cafeteria and see four African-American journalists sitting alone together, having lunch.

"I hate the hypocrisy," he complained of his colleagues. "*They* isolate themselves from *everyone else,* then complain about racism. *They're* being racist themselves."

Because *he* was feeling uncomfortable then, the white writer recalled, he walked over to the "all Black" group (his words), sat down and declared, "I'm integrating this table!"

Hurray for the good guy? Guess again.

Even with all those years of Civil Rights advocacy under his belt, at that moment that writer reverted to one of the most common expressions of everyday racism. First, he assumed that any time black people get together with one another, they do so for sinister, separatist reasons.

Wrong.

Black people have black friends and co-workers with whom they eat and socialize, like everyone else. It's ninety-nine percent likely that the four black journalists were friends who happened to eat together. As a white person, how many times have you been part of a social group made up exclusively of *white* people? Did you choose those companions only because they were white? How about the fact that maybe you've worked together, attended the same church, or played tennis together for several years?

Second, it was the white writer—not his black co-workers—who cast the situation in a racial light at all with his "integrating the table" comment. If he spotted a friend at the table, why not just sit down as he would had the group been white? Or, if he sensed the group's conversation was private, why not either ask if he could join them or respect their privacy, as he also would, had they been white?

Along this same line, a white supervisor in my building once warned a new black employee not to be seen "congregating" with other Blacks in the office. (There were damned few back then. Can three form a congregation?) The supervisor was vague about the reasons, telling the employee that it just "looked bad." What he really meant was that it looked threatening to him, and that any "all Black" group undermined "legitimate" structures in the workplace.

Admittedly, the reactions by the writer and the supervisor were largely gut-level human nature. No one wants to be rebuffed and excluded. We each look for the welcoming face, the friendly smile, and, among strangers in social settings, for the people who seem most likely to accept us. Because African Americans, other people of color, and white women often are rejected by white males in corporate and other settings, we sometimes tend to gravitate to one another. But it is not to shut other people out; rather, it is to create a safe, let-our-hair-down space for commiserating and relaxing .

"It's like family time," says writer Amoja Three Rivers. "We are not being against anybody by being for ourselves"—unlike the Klan and racially exclusive country clubs, for instance. When it comes to a group of black people sitting around talking or chatting at the water cooler, it helps to remember that:

- **A group of African-American people meeting or socializing in the workplace is as legitimate as a group of white guys,** a group of white women, a group of Presbyterians. They are not doing anything wrong, and they don't need a white person's permission or presence to "legitimize" them.
- **Black people coming together as a group are not shutting you out;** they are merely including themselves in. Probably no racial exclusion is intended. If you see a friend among them, sit down; or, if you want to join the group, ask. Don't make mindless comments, like, "Is this a caucus?"
- **A group of African-American colleagues meeting or socializing together poses no threat to you.** *If you feel threatened, it's your problem.* Ask yourself why you feel threatened. Do you distrust black people for some reason? Do you feel something lacking regarding your own cultural identity? Do you feel guilty because *your* social groups exclude African-American people?
- **If you see a friend among the black people in a group, you should feel just as comfortable taking a seat with that friend** as you would if you sought him or her out in a sea of white faces. Any paranoia on your part is your problem. African Americans need not modify their behavior and pander to your insecurities to make you feel more comfortable.
- **It is sheer narcissism to assume that African Americans meeting together or just sitting together are plotting the overthrow of you or the rest of white society,** or even making

negative comments about white people. Believe it or not, we also have families, lovers, career aspirations, bills, interior decorating, taxes, and life in general to discuss with one another.

...and Black Schools Are Not Racist

A majority of this nation's historically African-American colleges were founded with the help of grants and donations from white people— early liberals, in fact—who believed black people had a right to an education, but many of whom didn't want blacks sitting next to their sons and daughters in classrooms.

From the beginning, white racism—not black separatist sentiments— was the impetus for separate institutions. Historically black colleges have never been closed to white people, unlike many white institutions. Nearly all have some white students, faculty, and trustees. (Too bad the history of many predominantly white colleges doesn't share the same legacy. My father fought for his country in the Korean War, but was not allowed to attend the then all-white University of North Carolina on the GI Bill.) Black schools are not and could never be "racist" institutions even if they wanted to be, since they are subject to white-run governmental and educational accrediting regulations and borrow money from white-run banks for loans.

Are historically African-American schools needed today, now that our country is "integrated"? According to researchers Ernest T. Pascarella and Patrick T. Terenzini, a black undergraduate student has a significantly better chance of graduating from a historically black college than from a predominantly white one. An African-American graduate student I know has a professor who told her that black people never earned above a B in his class. Even if the professor did nothing overt to sabotage her, the fact that he planted seeds of doubt had to affect her performance negatively.

Likewise, sororities and fraternities with predominantly black memberships are generally not racist. Most grew out of a need for brotherhood and sisterhood, networking and a "who-you-know system" to give Blacks the same edge that Whites have in getting ahead. Several have a minority of white and other non-black members. Support and professional societies, such as the National Association of Black Journalists, are not "racist" either.

White people who balk at black support groups, professional organizations, and historically black colleges don't realize that white counterparts also exist—they make up the whole corporate, educational, social, and cultural structure of the United States.

"Some of My Best Friends"—
Beyond Adoring the Maid

It has always puzzled me to hear white people use the "some of my best friends are Black" line, presumably as a talisman against accusations of racism—mainly because, for too many of you, the statement is a bald-faced lie.

Among the dozens of people with whom I regularly come in contact, I have about a dozen close friends of various racial and ethnic origins. Among them are a few white people I trust and respect. Those friendships, like most others, come in the oddest fashion. One friend in particular is a puzzle to many of the white liberals at my office. Glenna is a self-styled political and theological white conservative from rural Tennessee. During her formative years, the only black people she ever saw were laborers who worked with her father. After a 1984 companywide racism workshop in which I was particularly dogmatic, Glenna walked up to me and said, "I'd like to be friends with you but I don't know how to talk to you. Everything I say you'd think is wrong."

I liked her honesty, so we talked. She explained to me that, growing up, "some of the best people" she ever knew were the families of her father's black co-workers. Whites and Blacks lived separately because that's just the way it was, but now she knows that "wasn't right."

Once Glenna and I began to be honest with one another about the artificial racial barriers society had erected between us, our real friendship built a bridge. Now, she hears all about my misadventures as a newlywed and my career dreams; I hear about problems with her daughter and her plans to build a new house. And because we're both human beings still growing beyond racism, we both blurt out whatever we think regarding race, and each trusts the other to set her straight. That's friendship.

Meanwhile, though, I've been *drafted* as "best friend" by several white liberals in our office, some of whom I barely know. A friend recently reported overhearing a white co-worker throw my name around as a "close friend" of hers after she was accused of being racist to her black secretary. I had been to lunch with this co-worker once, and had talked to her occasionally in the hall, but that was all.

The absurdity, hypocrisy, and futility of "best-friending" a black person to hide your own racism and elevate you in the eyes of Blacks and liberal Whites is best exposed by Mildred, a fictional black domestic worker who is the protagonist in a novel by Alice Childress. In one story, Mildred lays it on the line to her well-meaning, white liberal employer, who repeatedly insists that Mildred is "like one of the family."

> "In the second place, I'm *not* just like one of the family at all! The family eats in the dining room and I eat in the kitchen. Your mama borrows your lace tablecloth for her company and your son entertains his friends in your parlor.... You say, 'We don't think of her as a servant'... but after I have worked myself into a sweat cleaning the bathroom and the kitchen ... making the beds ... cooking the lunch ... washing the dishes and ironing Carol's pinafores ... I do not feel like no weekend house guest. I feel like a servant, and in the face of that I have been meaning to ask you for a slight raise which will ... make me know my work is appreciated" (Childress, p. 2).

No law says that a white liberal must have a certain number of African-American friends to maintain her or his liberal status. Society has separated us in many ways: by family groups and social class, into neighborhoods and churches, and even in the workplace. For better or worse, your best friends may *not* be Black. That's not a crime, and that doesn't make you racist. But faking superficial friendships in the name of liberalism can become a racist act.

If you have regular close encounters with people from other racial groups, however, allow those liaisons to help you work through residual racist stereotypes and practices. To strengthen and add substance to your interracial friendships and work relationships, it is important that you:

- **reexamine your inner circles at work and in other settings.** Do you ever have an opportunity to build close friendships with black people? (You can still be "liberal"—give to causes, advocate for black people on your job, question racist jokes and policies, vote responsibly—without necessarily having a black best friend.) You need to ask yourself, though, if you are avoiding or are afraid of black people, or why your social environments are racially exclusive.
- **examine not only your company's official policies, but also the "unwritten" ones.** Are black co-workers included in lunches and social hours where informal yet important decisions are often made? If you do invite black people into the "inner circle," do you tend to invite only "acceptable" black people (those who talk, look, or act "white" in your mind)?
- **advocate for people of color whenever the opportunity arises, not only when it is politically to your advantage.** Don't ever allow other white people to tell racist jokes or make racist comments to your face, even if the only other ones around are white folks.
- **ask an African-American friend or colleague whom you trust and respect to "pull your coat" if you do or say something racist.** (Choose a person who is on equal footing, though. Not many people are going to criticize the supervisor who signs their paychecks, their landlord, or their professor.) And if you ask for feedback and criticism, be prepared to take it. Don't argue, rationalize, or make excuses. Ponder what you're being told. Remember, you've asked your friend to be honest. And no one knows more about being black than a black person.

You Can Say These and Still Be Racist

1 "I can't be racist because I have a black best friend or have dated
black women or men, or have adopted a black or biracial child."
You can be racist. You can have an African-American wife or husband
and still automatically cross the street when you see a group of African-
American teenage boys approaching you on a lonely street. You can
love your black boyfriend and stab a black male co-worker in the back
if both of you are in line for the same promotion. All you have to do is
think, "Etta never said I was racist and she's my wife, so I must not be
racist," or "If only all blacks were like my boyfriend. . . ." (A white co-
worker and friend told me recently that she had never really warmed
to most black people, but liked me because I didn't act "too black,"
meaning my parents and my college education have given me a generic
accent and eclectic taste in music and art.)

2 "I can't be racist because I watch 'The Cosby Show.'" (I swear
someone said this at a 1992 Nashville city council meeting.) Same
principle as No. 1. That doesn't prove a thing. How would you feel if
your daughter brought a black fiancé home? What if an assertive black
woman became your supervisor?

3 "I can't be racist because I vote for liberal Democrats and give to
the NAACP and the United Negro College Fund." And I appreci-
ate it. However, white racism so permeates every level of life in America that you can forthrightly admire the Rev. Jesse Jackson from afar,
while you disparage Leroy Jackson, your African-American supervisor.
Again, racism at its strongest is not perpetrated maliciously by "bad"
people, but by those who think one good deed or one revolutionary
era during their college years—instead of a life-changing, ever-vigilant
approach—makes them immune. The road to full-blown racism is
paved with good intentions.

4 A white man posed this question to the late author James Baldwin:
"If Blacks suddenly came to power, they'd turn against and oppress

white people. What's to stop them from creating a black Hitler or black
Mussolini?" To which Baldwin replied, "What's your point? We sur-
vived the white Hitler and the white Mussolini."

For the record, the chance of African Americans in this country
"taking over" is unlikely for several reasons. We have neither the numbers nor the "manifest destiny" and "chosen race" rhetoric to spur us.
More important, in order to justify maintaining white racism, white
people often purposely translate our demands for justice and equality
into our wanting to "get back" at white people. Believe it or not, what
with raising families, working everyday, paying bills, and battling
racism at all levels of our lives, most of us don't even take the time to
vote when we should, much less worry about getting back at someone.
Survival with justice, not revenge against white Americans, is the primary agenda of most African Americans.

5 "I'm from north of the Mason-Dixon line (or New York City or
Chicago or Los Angeles), and I live and work in multi-ethnic settings, so I'm not racist." Or "I know it must be hard for you Blacks who
live in the South." This Northerners-are-more-liberal debate is a run-
ning point of tension between people in my company's main office in
Nashville and those in our New York office. As an African-American
woman reared in North Carolina, I know we've got many shameful,
brutal expressions of white racism in our Southern history: Strom
Thurmond and Jesse Helms; George Wallace and Bull Connor; the
Klan-Nazi murders in Greensboro; Medgar and Martin's assassinations;
the church bombings in Birmingham; the sit-ins in Nashville. But
we've also got more historically African-American colleges in the
South, more black homeowners, and lower unemployment rates for
African Americans living in the Sun Belt. Moreover, all the racially
motivated violence in the South of 1963 can't excuse or erase the
weight of perhaps less sensational but equally devastating white racism
in the "liberal" North of the 1990s. Racial violence? Can you say
"Howard Beach" and "Bensonhurst," New York? How about Rodney
King's beating by four valley cops in laid-back, ultra-cool Los Angeles?
Cabs in New York won't pick up an African-American man, and only

overpriced gypsy cabs run to Harlem most of the time. Northern white liberals perpetrate and benefit from racism as much, if not more than, their more conservative, Southern sisters and brothers. A poor, Louisiana dirt farmer in the Klan robe can't really hurt me; a Harvard-educated, self-proclaimed liberal boss from the Northeast, who pays a black woman sixty cents for every dollar a white male colleague earns, can.

6 **"I understand it's because of oppression and everything, but most drug dealers and thieves *are* black men."** No. Most criminals are white because white people are the majority. In fact, most African-American men are law-abiding citizens. They work, pay taxes, rear children, and contribute positively to their communities. The image of the hulking black robber, rapist, and murderer is largely the lore of a white society which chooses to make demons of the people it oppresses in order to justify that oppression.

But, yes, a disproportionately high number of black and Latino males *are* serving hard time in U.S. jails and prisons, many for the same crimes for which white perpetrators receive less severe sentences.

As writer Clarence Page says, "It is politically incorrect to suggest that the nation's criminal justice systems might be infected with a racial double standard [or] to talk about studies that indicate first-time juvenile white offenders are more likely to be referred to treatment or turned over to their parents than their black counterparts, who appear to be far more likely to be incarcerated for the same first-time offense."

PC: Politically Correct or Plain Courtesy
Why "Classical" Isn't; and, Never Say "Nigger" Again

"What do you mean when you say I'm rebellious
'Cause I don't accept everything that you're tellin' us?"

from "You Must Learn" by rapper KRS-One

"It's fact, not fiction
I use good diction
I've never been arrested for a criminal conviction"

from "Let Me Cool My Jets," unpublished rap lyric by Rupert Burton, 1990

To many African Americans like me, who came along during the Vietnam War and Woodstock, U.S. college campuses and the whole world of academia surrounding them have always seemed symbols of open-mindedness—breeding grounds for liberation struggles, protest marches, and questioning of the status quo.

It has therefore been disappointing to note the recent trend among many white academics to plug up their open minds each time people of color and women demand that their forgotten histories, languages, literature, and philosophies be given equal time in the classroom. Many noted white male academicians blanch at the mere mention of "multicultural curricula," "Afrocentric" education, or "feminist" theology. Arthur Schlesinger, Jr., an author with two Pulitzer Prizes to his credit, recently devoted a whole book to denouncing multicultural education as a threat to America's unity and values.

In *The Disuniting of America: Reflections on a Multicultural Society,* he calls the push for multicultural curricula and bilingual education in public schools a dangerous "revolt against the melting pot" that denies "the idea of a common culture and a single society." But African-American professor William Strickland of the University of Massachusetts at Amherst, translates Schlesinger's words a different way. He debunks claims that multicultural studies urge social fragmentation. (What, after all, is more fragmenting than the institution of slavery, which ripped apart black families and ultimately relegated them to racially segregated schools and communities?) In calling for more diverse studies, Strickland says, people of color are simply challenging white racism and the historically based fallacy of white superiority in the United States and around the world. The rebellion by white academic types boils down to "American in-house intellectuals circling the wagons" to protect the White American assumption "that all Americans are White, English-speaking descendants of Europe" (Strickland, p. 130).

In other words, the white backlash has erupted because many white people refuse to concede that their tradition, language, and notions of "classical" education—like every other icon of American life—are contaminated by racism, sexism, classism, ageism, handicapism and heterosexism.

Like it or not, however, our language and what we prize as "American" history and tradition belie white, male prejudices and myths designed purely to keep white males on top. "Firemen" still means "men." If you don't believe it, read the newspapers and count the number of discrimination and harassment lawsuits filed by women firefighters and police officers who catch hell for breaking gender barriers.

Or read the encyclopedia entry on "classical" music. Classical music is not Muddy Waters, Ella Fitzgerald, Appalachian folk songs, or slave spirituals—though spirituals are among the earliest truly American forms. "Classical" music is Beethoven, Chopin, Wagner, and those other high-brow white guys and their modern-day counterparts.

Look at a dictionary or a scientific research journal and discover that what becomes "tradition," "reality," and "scientifically sound" has everything to do with where you come from and what color your skin is. Even "objective" information is subject to the whims of racism. Says writer Calvin Morris, "Since Blacks [and other people of color] were considered ordained by nature to be less than Whites in every way, white power [has] sought to institutionalize that 'truth' into the very fabric of American life" (Morris, p. 21).

So now, as formerly repressed groups grow more assertive in redefining themselves and shedding the labels historically *imposed* upon them, the white powers-that-be cry foul in defense of "clarity," national "unity," and respect for "proper English." At best, white critics poke fun at the "pettiness" of "P. C. police," like talk show host Rush Limbaugh's dismissal of women's rights activists as "feminazis." At worst, African-American studies professors are called "fascists," the practice of challenging sexist language dubbed "oppressive," and the push for inclusiveness denounced as having "gone too far." Even many white liberals draw the line of progressive thinking at changing "traditional" language and concepts of history and literature, arguing that "historic context" is more important than abandoning lies and setting records straight.

Just remember this the next time you roll your eyes and balk at language sensitivities that "go too far": *One person's politically correct "crap" is another person's reality.*

Or, as *Ms.* magazine editor Robin Morgan puts it, "If choosing inclusive language instead of carelessly cruel terminology [and curricula] that gives pain to others is 'P. C.,' then P. C. must stand for 'plain courtesy.' [And] expanding the perimeter of scholarship so that the contributions of the majority of humanity are represented must then be 'C. S.': common sense, because it would benefit us all" (Morgan, p. 1).

True, the push for inclusiveness is not always pleasant. It can be a little annoying when a self-righteous do-gooder makes a show of her or his sensitivity—especially when that person feels the need to correct others at inappropriate times, or use it to flaunt his or her progressiveness. (I have one friend who insists upon calling my husband my "life companion." It drives Larry nuts, and he always fumes, "I'm her husband, dammit!")

And even some of us from repressed groups have become so accustomed to oppressive, "normal" language that we can be as hostile as some purist white folks when challenged to alter it. (In other words, don't look for *consensus* among African Americans, other people of color, and white women about "correct" language and concepts, because you won't find it. I grit my teeth in my hometown church when our black preacher asks God to forgive our sins and make us "white as snow." "Just don't bleach *me,* Jesus," I pray. "I'm perfectly satisfied with my maple brown.")

But, despite lack of consensus, I've found that it is better for white people—and all people—to err on the side of being too sensitive with regard to "correct" language. In terms of forging stronger relationships with people of color and overcoming racism, it can't hurt. And, once the words get into your consciousness, you'll find that some of that sensitivity spills over into your actions.

A comprehensive, straightforward guide to cleaning up racist and sexist language is *The Nonsexist Word Finder: A Dictionary of Gender-Free Usage,* by Rosalie Maggio (Boston: Beacon Press, 1988). I also recommend *Guidelines for Selecting Bias-Free Textbooks and Storybooks* from the Council on Interracial Books for Children in New York. Don't let the title fool you. It's an indispensable guide for adults—teachers, playwrights, movie critics, news editors, advertising agents, corporate types—who live and work in multiracial settings).

The following is an abbreviated list of my personal suggestions about racist words and phrases to watch for. No one expects radical changes overnight, but take heart and keep trying. Remember, the leap your ancestors made from "nigra" and "colored" to "Negro" was also tough.

When You're Talking About *Us*

1 When referring to people of African descent in the United States, use the terms "Black" or "African American" or Afro-Caribbean and Haitian, or Dominican, etc. Elementary as this may seem, I still hear "colored" used by white people I wrongly assume should know better. "Negro" (chances of "mispronunciation" are too great) and "colored" are *out* except when they are part of a proper name or if you're quoting history texts. (Or if you're referring to the ludicrously strident racial categories formerly used in South Africa.)

2 Don't say to someone, "You don't act Black or talk Black." This is *not* a compliment. Don't assume that a strong Western work ethic,

attention to "proper" English, and a college education are for Whites only. As for "acting Black" or "talking Black," what is usually meant is some stereotype white people hold about the way African Americans dress, think, act, speak, vote. We are not monolithic, though; we are individuals, as different as Gloria Steinem is from David Duke. And, as I said earlier, *all people have accents* shaped by speech patterns from our respective communities. If Hattie McDaniel had an accent, so does anchorman Dan Rather.

3 By the same token, **don't assume that intelligence, "success" in a corporate environment, and high grade-point average are due to anything other than gifts from God and nose-to-the-grindstone hard work.** A co-worker once asked me if I had any white people in my "family background." When I looked at her the way she deserved to be looked at, she said, "Well, you're just so articulate." *It was not a compliment.*

In an editorial in the October 2, 1989, issue of *Newsweek,* an African-American woman explained it this way: "For many of us [African Americans], life is a curious series of encounters with white people who want to know why we [middle- and upper-income, "articulate," and/or socially responsible black people] are 'different' from other Blacks—when, in fact, most of us are only 'different' from the common, negative images of black life" (Raybon, p. 11).

Author Gar Anthony Haywood also advises against describing African Americans who excel in science and arts, for example, as "exceptional," "atypical," or "fortunate" enough to have benefitted from affirmative action. He recommends: "Use the terms 'hard work,' 'diligent,' and 'self-sacrificing' whenever possible. In other words, pretend you're talking about Larry Bird." Or Abraham Lincoln.

4 **Never say "nigger" again.** *Never* have I heard this word spoken by a white person—or a black one, for that matter—without feeling terribly angry and uncomfortable. Too much history and hostility are conjured up by this word. (The same goes for other racial slurs, such as "coon," "porch monkey," or "jig.") I don't care how you use it. I don't care if you're quoting some horrible white racist you abhor—*do* *not say it,* and confront those white people who do. Say "the n-word" or "a racial slur" if you have to; it may sound silly or stilted, but you may save a relationship with an African-American friend or colleague. If a black friend says she doesn't mind you saying it, she's lying.

Gar Anthony Haywood again offers sage advice about using the word "nigger":

> Don't say it, write it, or sing it in any key, including B-flat. Don't use it as a 'sounds like' clue in charades or a six-letter word in Scrabble, and if the opportunity ever presents itself, don't sign it for the deaf.

Yes, I know some Blacks use it to describe one another—as either a term of endearment or, most times, of derision. That's partly historic self-hatred taught to us by Whites. As our awareness grows, many black celebrities, like comedian Richard Pryor, have dropped the word from their comedy movies and stand-up acts because they realize how painful and self-destructive it is.

5 **We are people too,** so make sure that references to us do not false- ly and unnecessarily suggest otherwise. Saying "Blacks and women," for example, implies that black women are not also women. Instead, say "black people and white women" or "black men and women of all racial groups." You get the idea. In a recent newspaper article on the U. S. South, the writer said, "Americans view Southerners . . . as 'a little less intelligent, a little less hard-working' than Whites in general, according to social scientist Tom Smith." What's wrong with this state- ment? It sounds like all Southerners are white people. (It also sounds like "Southerners" aren't also "Americans.")

Such statements seem to separate "we" from "they," and again make white Americans the norm and other racial groups the aberration. News media are notorious for saying things like, "Nashville homeown- ers fear black migration" or "Democrats court the black vote," as if there were no black homeowners in Nashville, or black Democrats. African Americans and other people of color in this nation are not only people of color, but also Americans, Democratic and Republican vot- ers, and homeowners.

6 **Two-thirds of the world is not a minority.** Two-thirds of the world's human inhabitants are descendants of African, Asian, Middle Eastern, Latino, South Pacific and Native/Aleutian people. The U. S. Census shows that by the year 2000 white Americans will, in fact, be a racial minority. The word "minority" for "nonwhites" doesn't ring true.

So what do we use as an omnibus expression? It's not easy. Our agency uses the phrase "racial-ethnic persons" to refer to people formerly called "minorities." This is imprecise, however, because *all* people—including white people—have racial and ethnic identities. I prefer the term "people of color" because it draws the distinction without making a value judgment on the basis of numbers ("minority") or normalcy ("nonwhite" implies that "white" is the standard and any other group is an aberration).

7 **Assume that any African American or other person of color is "qualified" until proven otherwise.** If some white employers abuse affirmative action by bringing in underqualified black people, it may be *racist*, but it is not *reverse racism*. In the long term, the black employee is the one most hurt because she or he has been set up to fail. And white folks never let us forget it. I'm still hearing about a black writer employed by (and subsequently dismissed from) our agency ten years ago. The story goes that the writer was so incompetent that the bosses were "scared to hire another one" until me. Meanwhile, incompetent white workers come and go—and some are promoted—without any ridiculous, sweeping comments about the incompetency of white people in general.

Newspaper columnist Anna Quindlen reminds us that, "The stories about the incompetent black co-worker always leave out two things: the incompetent white co-workers and the talented black ones."

8 **Black people are *not* "taking over"** at your job, in the cities, in your neighborhood, or anywhere else, so don't say it. In her *Guide to Cultural Etiquette*, Amoja Three Rivers asserts that notions about black people taking over "are myths put out and maintained by the ones who really have. It is a conscious and time-honored tactic for the white, straight, gentile males at the top to create situations in which the rest of us are encouraged to blame each other for our respective oppression," she writes. "Don't fall for it" (Three Rivers, p. 7). Adds Quindlen:

> The opponents of affirmative action programs say they are opposing the rank unfairness of preferential treatment. But there was no great hue and cry when colleges were candid about wanting to have geographic diversity, perhaps giving the kid from Montana an edge. There has been no national outcry when legacy applicants whose transcripts were supplemented by Dad's alumni status—and cash contributions to the college—were admitted over more qualified comers. We somehow only discovered that life was not fair when the beneficiaries happened to be Black.

If you're seeing more African Americans now in your place of business, in social clubs, and other settings, it's only because, after four hundred years, we're taking small steps toward correcting racial injustice in our homeland. And we've far from made it. As of 1991, the U. S. had more college-age African-American men in prisons than on campuses. Of 127,000 students enrolled in law school in 1991, only 7,500 were African American. Only three percent of all doctors in this country are Black.

9 Watch for loaded words like "militant," "gang," "tribe," "primitive," "ghetto," etc. In a recent editorial on urban issues, the writer—a white woman—referred to a black California congresswoman as "militant" because the congresswoman confronted former U. S. President George Bush about his lack of concern for U. S. cities. Two years before, the same writer had criticized Bush's aggressive posture in the Gulf War, remarking on his 1991 "kick his ass" comment about Iraqi leader Saddam Hussein. But she never referred to Bush as "militant."

Your words can smack of racism. Before you use a word like "militant" to describe the words or actions of a black person, ask yourself if you'd apply it to a white person. If a congresswoman representing her urban constituents is militant because of her verbal aggressiveness, then surely the President of the United States saying he's going to use military force to "kick" another world leader's "ass" is militant. If the Black Panthers were militant, then white parents in Little Rock and Boston who staged violent protests against school desegregation were militant.

If black youth just hanging out on the corner are a "gang," so are white suburban kids hanging out at the mall. Poor people live in neighborhoods and communities, just like you. Think before you dismiss where they live as a "ghetto." And all people derive from tribal groups—Europe has as "primitive" a history as any other part of the world.

10 **Think twice before you use "black" or "dark" as negative adjectives,** as in a "black day," a "black heart," or say things like "Things are not as black as they seem." According to antibias activist Louise Derman-Sparks, "Just speaking English teaches differential values for whiteness and blackness." She notes forty-four positive meanings for whiteness in the average dictionary, compared with sixty negative ones for blackness (Derman-Sparks, p. 4).

The words "black" and "dark" historically have conjured up foreboding and evil in white people's vernacular, while "white" and "fair" are equated with purity and cleanliness. Consider "black magic." Or a "black lie" versus a "little white lie." Those color comparisons have found their way into our notions of race, as well. A person who is "fair of face" is white and, therefore, beautiful. Biblical allusions—historically translated for us by Europeans—equate purity with being "white as snow." Rethink those usages. What about "white as death" or "white as leprosy"? Because color words are so racially loaded, try to avoid them and don't teach them to your children. Say "a dirty lie" or "a little lie." Say "a cruel heart" or "a horrible day."

11 **Do not ever call elderly African-American men "boys" or African-American women "girls".** You should know the history. Since slavery, white people have often purposely demeaned black men—from pullman porters to federal judges—by calling them "boy." Former United Nations Ambassador Andrew Young, an African American, tells a stunning story about a white woman at his hotel who mistook him for a bellman, addressed him as "boy," and requested that he carry her bags. He was there to deliver a keynote address to a global conference. Calling grown people "boy" and "girl" can be classist as well as racist: many white, upper-income homemakers refer to the fifty-year-old black, Latina or white woman who comes in to clean as "my girl." I had to hotly correct a twenty-five-year-old white nurse at a hospital who scolded my eighty-year-old godmother, saying "Now, Mary, you be a good girl!" This is just plain disrespectful for *any* older adult, and especially for older African Americans who remember the days when white people regularly and publicly denigrated them.

For many African Americans, it is not a sign of "chumminess" when white strangers are too familiar with them. Because many Whites traditionally showed us little respect, African Americans have compensated by being more formal with one another—especially with our elders. I was raised to call my pastor "Reverend Tolbert," and older adults are Mrs., Miss, Mr., Uncle or Aunt. My mother goes ballistic when she hears some white children call their parents by their first names. (That practice is not common among American families, but once is too many to my "Muh.")

Unless you're a *friend* of the person in question, use a courtesy title and her or his last name. You may subsequently be invited to call a person by her or his first name, but *wait for the invitation.*

12 When greeting an African American, **don't imitate things you've heard in rap songs or B movies.** In other words, you do not have to yelp, "What's happening, my man?" "Hey, Bro!" "Word up!" or "What it is, my Sistuh?" You don't have to slap us five or bump rumps with us. Sure, many people use slang indigenous to their respective hometowns, schools, and neighborhoods, but not all black people talk like a rap star. Besides, we're bilingual. We understand, "How are you? My name is . . ."

13 Do not argue with an African American about what offends and what is appropriate address for African Americans in general. A white male friend once argued me down, claiming that it didn't bother his "other black friends" to be called "nigger" in jest. He also assured me that "all the brothers [black men] like Schlitz Malt Liquor," adding, "I've been around enough black people to know."

No one knows more about being black than black people, whether they live on Central Park West or in a shantytown in Mud Slat, Mississippi. I don't care what you've read, where you marched or worked while in the Peace Corps, whom you married, or how many black friends you have. What your own black friends may tolerate—or claim that they tolerate—other African Americans may not abide. As I said earlier, black people come in all types. There are black Muslims, atheists, Buddhists, Christians and Jews; black doctors, lawyers, stock brokers and prison inmates; black college professors, nuclear scientists, environmental activists and feminist theologians. But we all have one thing in common: we all know more about African-American preferences and experiences than any white folks do.

14 Do not blithely equate the African-American experience with the oppression suffered by any other people, especially white Americans. Although oppressed and marginalized people all have their war stories, the African-American experience is unlike any other in *this* nation. The stories of other groups should be honored and remembered and learned by all, but it dishonors all oppressed people to compare, subsume or lump together, for example, the Jewish Holocaust, the Native American "Trail of Tears," African-American slavery, and Japanese-American internment. Each stands alone as an unconscionable page in human history. And each offers a unique lesson for our society.

But when it comes to modern-day, American racism on a personal, gut level, African Americans still are considered the most "aberrant" group in U. S. culture. I have a girlfriend whose Japanese mother (married to her white father) looked askance at her daughter when she brought me home for the first time. "Never marry a black man," her mother told Kim. "You will disgrace us." A Native American friend told me she preferred to date men of other races, but not black men— because "my mom would kill me." In my favorite television show of the

1970s—"The High Chaparral"—the white ranch owner was married to a Latina. Face it, the show never would have seen daylight if the woman had been African American.

And I still remember an interview televised during the 1950s uproar over school desegregation in Arkansas, in which a white female student said she'd rather attend classes with Chinese immigrants than black Americans because the "Chinese are more like *us*" than black people, who had shared her language and history.

15 Never make sweeping criticisms about black people to black co-workers and friends; and if you do, certainly don't expect their assent. Don't say to your African-American co-worker, "Isn't it horrible the way black men use drugs and desert their families?" First of all, that is a stereotype—some black men use drugs and/or desert their families, but so do some white men. Secondly, you're in no position to make generalizations about black people, because odds are you've not been immersed in the black experience.

16 Allow for the possibility that two different African Americans may have two different views, even of race relations and racism. If you hear opposing views on a subject from African Americans, listen and learn from all of them (think of the Bush-Clinton-Perot race of 1992). No one tells white feminists and white Klansmen, for example, that they need to get their act together so we'll have an easier view of the "white" agenda. Why hold Blacks to the same impossible ideal? As you encounter them, treat people as individuals: if one black colleague prefers to be called "African American," while another prefers "Black"— if racial delineations are necessary at all—respect the individual. Putting diverse people in one category or box for your convenience is racist. Period.

I have several friends named Robert. One prefers to be called "Bob," the other "Bobby," the other "RK," and the last "Robert." The same principle applies to perceptions, preferences, and opinions about racial issues. Yes, we are African Americans, but that's not all we are.

17 Our hair is not "nappy" or "kinky." It is simply our hair, not to be compared to or measured against white people's hair or anyone else's hair. African Americans' noses aren't "wide" and our lips aren't "thick," unless you're using European characteristics as the measuring stick. Don't. If we were to disparage from *our* point of view, we'd call white people's lips "thin," their noses "pinched" or "pug," and their hair "stringy." It's all relative. "Nude" and "flesh-colored" bandages, acne medicine, panty hose, and make-up are only nude on beige or taupe-colored people. *Your* norms are not *the* norms, no matter how much this society caters to white people. Such norms are merely *your* reality, not *the* reality. The rest of us are under no obligation to accept them.

When talking about yourself

18 Rethink your use of words like "classical," "standard," and "traditional" in describing forms of music, literature, and theological and philosophical understandings. What is usually meant are ideas and arts promulgated by white, Western males—the deader the better.

As one of the earliest indigenous American music forms, African slave spirituals are classical. Jazz by Miles Davis and Dizzy Gillespie is also classical. Phyllis Wheatley and Langston Hughes wrote classical poetry and fiction—to African Americans, at least. The point is, just because white, Western scholars have thrown the words "classical" and "traditional" around doesn't mean they own them. True, works of some white men may have great merit, but in a global context—in a world free of long-standing racism and cultural imperialism—the contributions to literature, arts and science by people of color and women would be equally valuable.

"PRESIDENT?... NO, CHILD, BUT YOU CAN GROW UP TO BE FRONT-RUNNER!"

The Trouble With Elvis and Larry Bird

When Imitation is *Not* the Sincerest Form of Flattery

"Elvis was a hero to most
  but he never meant shit to me"
  from "Fight the Power," by rappers Public Enemy, 1989

"It is no accident that the source of 'hip' is the Negro, for he has been living
  on the margin between totalitarianism and democracy for two centuries."
  from The White Negro, *by Norman Mailer, 1957*

When the Elvis Presley commemorative stamp came out a while ago, white people in Nashville went stark-staring crazy. I couldn't walk into the post office without passing women joyfully hugging packets of "the King's" stamps to their hearts. About the fifth time I flat-out, indignantly refused to accept Elvis stamps from an astonished (then insulted) white postal clerk, I realized another chapter of this book was staring me in the face.

Imitation is the sincerest form of flattery? That might be true if your best girlfriend copies your hairstyle, or if college buddies buy the same starter jacket. But when it comes to white "pop" heroes, such as singers and sports figures, the realities of white racism historically have undermined sincerity.

White Americans are often surprised that many African Americans refuse to join the throng of those who worship white "soul" musicians, from Elvis Presley and Pat Boone to Vanilla Ice and New Kids on the Block. They similarly gripe that any black person who doesn't worship basketball great Larry Bird is just jealous or is "racist in reverse." But if it seems that white heroes are not getting their due from people of color, much of the blame rests with the frenzied white-dominated media and white fans. The problem with these heroes, frankly, is that white obsession with them often has more to do with our country's pathological negation of black people, and wanting to "one-up" the achievements of African Americans, than it does with the white performers' actual abilities—loath as many white Americans are to admit it.

Pat Boone's rendition of "Tooty Fruity" sold nearly twice as many copies as the original by black rhythm-and-blues great Little Richard. Is that honestly because Pat's was better? Elvis and his promoters themselves frequently admitted that his music was merely a "whitenized" version of early Chuck Berry and Little Richard "rock-n-roll" (a '50s black euphemism for having sex). Yet white women cried, threw panties on stage and fainted when Elvis swaggered on stage. Not much of an actor, he nonetheless sang his way to a fortune thanks to movies built around his aw-shucks troubadour. And the frenzy continues, years after his death. Almost every week the Nashville paper carries a story about another Elvis sighting. (The man is dead, okay?)

I'll admit that Elvis was cute when he was young. I know *I* never missed one of his movies (until I was about fourteen). So, before you get into a passion, understand that it is perfectly all right to be liberal and dig Elvis.

However, there's no denying that what pushed Elvis out front of Berry and Richard was, without a doubt, his Whiteness. And if you don't know the history or "just never thought about it," try doing some research. Historic television news footage shows 1950s and 1960s parents decrying "nigger rock-and-roll." White radio stations banned black songs; black artists who did manage some crossover appeal sold albums with cover photos of white lovers so as not to offend white fans with black faces.

The only way white kids in the '50s could indulge in the lively rhythms of "black" music and also live in polite (read white) society was to have a traditionally African-American sound encased in a safe, white artist. God forbid that white teenagers—particularly white girls—would publicly celebrate black men like Chuck Berry and Little Richard as their musical idols and sex symbols. Fresh-faced white artists who could mimic a "black" sound, however poorly (Pat Boone? Please!), became the bankable alternative for Whites who wanted to bop and be socially correct (for the 1950s) at the same time. So, we have Elvis and Pat Boone and Bill Haley and the Comets as "kings" of rock and roll, and James Brown, Berry and Richard as court jesters at best.

In a society that claims to celebrate originality—dare any modern band to declare itself "better than the Beatles," and see what kind of backlash you get from *Rolling Stone*—it seems hypocritical that white imitators most times get more media attention, sell more records and get more movie and commercial endorsement deals than the black originators of the sounds and moves. When it comes to black and white, many white people would rather reward mediocrity than give African-American innovators their due. They'd rather live a white lie than celebrate a black truth. Originality is only sacred if it performs in whiteface.

Things haven't changed much since Pat Boone and Elvis with regard to black music, white artists. When rap music burst on the scene in the late 1970s and 1980s as one of the freshest, most unapologetically African-American expressions of urban life in America, white youth flocked en masse to concerts and record stores. Although few truly understood the streetwise, revolutionary sentiments expressed by many rappers, white kids were intrigued by the outcry rap evoked from white adults who feared the audacious lyrics and the angry swagger of rap artists. The kids also loved the hard sound, the flagrant sexuality, the funky clothes, the slang, the irreverent and arrogant tone.

Rap quickly replaced rock as the music that shocked teenagers' parents. Rock suddenly became "establishment" music. Face it—Mick Jagger's pushing fifty. He's *our* generation, not *theirs*. Eric Clapton has turned introspective; Rod Stewart sings to cherubs about family values in his music videos. You don't hear much from the Dead anymore. It's rap's Public Enemy, Ice Cube, and Queen Latifah who are calling for riots in the streets, for resistance to racism, for boycott of White-washed Hollywood movies. As the most socially radical, politically relevant music of this age, rap has become this generation's rebel yell.

For white parents who feared the death of family values due to rap music (this fear of wanton, black musical influence on innocent white kids predated slavery, romped through the early 1900s' Black Bottom,

Savoy Stomp and juke joints, right on through Chuck Berry's double entendres and pre-Elvis hip-swivelling), crossover rappers like Hammer became likable alternatives, the middle ground. White parents seemed comforted by Hammer-like messages of Christianity ("Pray") melded with harmless conceit ("U Can't Touch This" and "2 Legit 2 Quit").

But as black rappers began to exert too much influence over white kids and over the economics of the music market, as cutting-edge music again became the black performer's domain, white promoters and performers decided to pull another Elvis, and find Whites who could imitate the sound and the moves, and still be "safe" sex symbols for white youth.

So the rap single that sold best in 1990 was by white rapper Vanilla Ice, whom at least one deejay sarcastically called "the Ricky Nelson of rap." Insipid though it was, promotion and sales of Vanilla Ice's single "Ice, Ice Baby" outstripped those of every black rapper that year, and he had a motion picture debut before most people learned his real name.

The same is true of the white "soul" group New Kids on the Block, a rip-off of earlier black, bubble-gum soul groups like the Jackson Five and New Edition. The New Kids phenomenon was even more offensive to me because, in at least one interview, the Kids publicly denied the primary influence of any black artists on their work—though they sounded more like New Edition than New Edition did. One member was quoted as saying that his major influences were European classical. (Roll over, Beethoven.)

And the list of successful imitators of black music goes on and on. White Britisher George ("I Want Your Sex") Michael regularly sweeps the rhythm-and-blues category at the Grammys and the American Music Awards; Michael Bolton covered Otis Redding's "Sittin' on the Dock of the Bay" and Percy Sledge's "When A Man Loves A Woman," and white people went ape, as if these songs were brand new.

The blatant negation of the influence, talent, and worthiness of black artists frankly rankles the African-American community, and makes it hard for black people to embrace your heroes while ours are ignored. Of course, the beauty of music is that it can transcend racial and cultural divisions *when musical influences are shared and credit to mentors is duly given.* But the fact is, while white critics and reviewers are quick to point out the white influences on against-the-grain black artists (How much has been written about the white, folk influences on black folk artist Tracy Chapman, or the "unusual" country flair displayed by black country great Charley Pride?), white artists are seldom held to the same courtesies of paying court to black musical pioneers.

That denial is not merely morally insulting, but it also means that white artists get rich by plagiarizing at the expense of black innovators. Or as James Ledbetter wrote in the 1992 premiere issue of *Vibe* magazine:

> Whites have been "riffing" off—or *ripping* off—black cultural forms for more than a century, and making a lot more money from them. Whether it's Al Jolson, Elvis, the Rolling Stones, Blues Brothers, Commitments, New Kids or Beasties, it's impossible to deny that, as a rule, the market responds much better to a black sound with a white face.

A notable exception to the rip-off artist mentality is white blues artist Bonnie Raitt, who adamantly tributes her black mentors, such as John Lee Hooker and Ruth Brown. She also features them on her albums and on tours, and she pays them. Quoted in *Jet* magazine, Raitt explained why white artists should pay homage to black mentors: "It would be dirty music for me to keep the money and not do something to try to pay them back. I don't think that we [Whites] can all sit here and sing rhythm and blues and not acknowledge or share our wealth with the artists who invented it. It's like stealing."

That America often ignores and negates black heroes has likewise made many African-American sports fans reluctant to join the throngs who worshiped recently retired basketball great Larry Bird of the Boston Celtics. True, he's an outstanding player. But I've been to Celtics games in Boston, and have overheard white people celebrating the fact that Bird has kept "niggers from taking over" the game.

In the case of Larry Bird, too, white racism goes way beyond brainless statements by ignorant individuals. Unfortunately for Bird—a true sports hero, in many ways—white racism became a bulwark of the pro-

Bird frenzy. In 1979, when both Bird and friend-rival Earvin "Magic" Johnson were rookies in the NBA, Johnson led the Los Angeles Lakers to the NBA championship against Philadelphia. Although Johnson, an African American, had played guard during the whole season, he became emergency center after Kareem Abdul Jabbar broke his hand in the final game. Johnson scored forty-two points, and the Lakers won the championship.

Even with those heroics, who was named NBA Rookie of the Year? Larry Bird. True, Bird also played well that year, but Magic practically won the championship single-handedly. When it comes to Bird, Ice, New Kids, and Elvis, it's as if the very reason Whites revere these heroes is *because* they are white, and because they save white folks from having to pay tribute to outstanding, innovative African Americans.

And, Lord, don't let the situation be reversed. When black baseball star Hank Aaron broke Babe Ruth's home-run record, a number of white sports fans and sports writers cried foul and disavowed the legitimacy of Aaron's feat, citing technicalities such as Aaron's having more seasons than Ruth to beat the record. Many white baseball fans issued death threats against Hank Aaron.

Good for goose—screw the gander.

This white-imitation-is-better phenomenon is evident in other realms. Recently, a beauty magazine article revealed that, with the advent of white actress Michelle Pfeiffer, supermodel Cindy Crawford, and white soul singer Taylor Dane, white women are flocking to plastic surgeons to get their lips made fuller. Fashion-wise, thin Bette Davis lips are out; full, pouty lips are in. It is to laugh. I was in high school when a white schoolmate first called me "bubble lip," making fun of my full, African lips. Later, in college, I heard a white student call a black student "Ubangi lips" during an argument in the cafeteria. Broad, African noses are still denounced by some Whites as "coffee-coolers."

But suddenly three white women with full lips make the scene, and full lips become a fashion commodity. Shades of Bo Derek, who wore cornrows in one movie and was credited with "originating" a trend African women have worn for hundreds of years. Is no trend "legitimate" until popularized by white people?

All right already, you're saying. What can you do about all this stuff? Unless you're a media or music mogul, you can't counter millions of dollars of hype for less-deserving white celebrities. However, at the very least:

- **Don't think of listing rock-and-roll and soul "legends" without first mentioning Ray Charles, Chuck Berry, James Brown, and Little Richard before you even *discuss* Elvis.** Don't call Elvis the "king of rock-and-roll"—the "king of *white people's* rock-and-roll" is okay, if you must crown him. While Elvis sold millions of records and made an indelible impression on music history, it's high time we set the record straight. This doesn't mean you can't groove to your old 45s or celebrate Elvis's birthday or collect the stamps. Just do so with your sense of history in order.

- Don't be a snot about it, but if the opportunity ever presents itself, **gently and firmly correct misconceptions voiced by friends and colleagues.** If you're talking with fellow music buffs and you know a relevant fact, spring it on them to make the conversation interesting. For example, say, "Yeah, I loved Elvis's movies, too. But did you know 'Hound Dog' was written and first recorded by a black woman named Big Mama Thornton? It's an interesting contrast."

- In choosing your musical and athletic heroes, **understand and acknowledge your racial biases. Explore new music and art forms from other ethnic communities** or socially conscious or interracial groups. (My personal favorites are Bruce Hornsby and the Range, Arrested Development, Johnny Clegg and Savuuka from South Africa, Special AKA, Garth Brooks, James Taylor, Tuck and Patti, Queen Latifah, Salt-n-Pepa, Tracy Chapman, 3rd Bass, Nancy Griffith.)

   Of course, your first criteria will be your own musical tastes and preferences—it *is* entertainment, after all—but attempt to broaden yourself. You might like what you hear and see. Raised in an Aretha-and-Temptations household, I nonetheless have added James Taylor, Goosecreek Symphony, Boston Camerata, Bonnie Raitt, Fleetwood Mac, the B-52s, and Steeleye Span to my "all-time favorites" list, thanks to exposure through white college pals. I hope the contributions were mutual.

- **Write letters of concern** to television networks, newspapers, and magazines that run articles or air stories about the popular music and sports legends that exclude major black personalities. Call them on poor research if nothing else.
- **Celebrate athletic legends and heroes from a variety of racial groups** (from Bird and Jabbar to Moon and Montana), and encourage your children to understand the concept of a "team" and to root for a team. Individual heroes are wonderful, but models of community spirit go a long way in helping people understand that sports figures are only as great as the teammates around them.
- **Emphasize athletes, musicians and other "pop" heroes who have broken racial, gender, and other barriers, as well as those who are positive role models** because of their personal habits (drug-free, philanthropists, returned to school to get a degree, spend time at children's hospitals, volunteer for national health and other committees). Teach your children that "hero" means more than the number of records sold, the slickest dance moves, the baddest Jaguar coupe, or the most points scored. Stress community responsibility, self-determination, and a positive attitude.

How Black People Abet White Racism

Including the Politics of Hair Texture and Skin Color

> "Like a guess I figure you to play some jigaboo
> On the plantation, what else can you do
> And Black women in this profession
> As for playin' a lawyer, out of the question
> For what they play, Aunt Jemima is the perfect term
> Even if now she got a perm"
>
> *from "Burn, Hollywood Burn," by Public Enemy, 1990*

Historically, because it has often been detrimental to our careers and livelihood—and life-threatening in some cases—many African Americans have often avoided direct confrontation with Whites about racism. Instead, we have sometimes turned our feelings of powerlessness, depression, and anger about white racism against one another in destructive ways, including:

1 **Exploiting and oppressing one another,** evident in the escalating rate of drive-by shootings, gang wars and illegal drug trade perpetrated by African-American criminals against the African-American community; gay-bashing within the black community; the growing number of African-American men who refuse to be financially and emotionally responsible to lovers, wives and children; and black parents who abuse their children.

2 **Dating or marrying white people as a "status symbol" because one believes White is "better than."** Misguided white liberals, like television and movie writers, often abet this self-hatred. NBC's progressive drama "L. A. Law" tackled social issues with stunning depth. Yet, the only people of color in the cast (one black attorney and two

Latino ones played by actors Blair Underwood, Jimmy Smits, and A. Martinez, respectively) all had on-screen romances with white women. (For the Latinos, white women were their *only* love interests). While the show's writers may congratulate themselves on "breaking down barriers," they actually exacerbated self-deprecation among people of color. Is the message that a man of color who "makes it" in corporate America must have a white woman on his arm as the ultimate symbol of achievement? Or are we supposed to rejoice that racism has subsided to the point that black men are free to pursue their "dream" of dating white women (a more sophisticated version of the stereotype of the black and brown male studs who secretly lust after the pure, white paragon of feminine beauty)? Either way, it's racist. While I applaud and support partners in interracial romances based on mutual attraction, love, and respect, I reject the notion that marrying or dating a white person somehow elevates the black partner.

3 **Using racist and other epithets to refer to one another**—when one black person calls another "nigger," or when a black man refers to a black woman (or any woman) as "bitch," " 'ho' " (whore), "hoochie," "skeezer," etc., or when black women constantly complain about "trifling, no-good black men" or call them "dogs."

4 **Using racial epithets against white people or against other people of color** and agreeing with white people who say things like, "Koreans are taking over," or "Puerto Ricans are ruining the neighborhood," or "Why can't they speak American?"

As for speaking "American," African-American brothers and sisters, how many of you are fluent in Kiowa, Cherokee, Oneida, Nez Perce or Ute?

5 **Denying or being shamed by one's own racial identity, either by surgery or assertion** (see the succeeding section on hair texture and skin color). This practice dates back to slavery, when some African Americans born with like-White features "passed" for White to escape racial oppression. Remember the hit movie *Imitation of Life?*

In recent years, media have covered stories of light-skinned African-American celebrities, contrasting those who wear their African and bi-cultural heritages proudly (superstar Lena Horne and actors Mario Van Peebles, Halle Berry, and Jasmine Guy) with others who deny it. "King of pop" and philanthropist Michael Jackson has made headlines for years by having his traditionally African features altered—nose nar-rowed, hair straightened, and skin lightened (he claims his skin color is caused by a rare disease). It may be mere speculation that Jackson is trying to distance himself from or obliterate his Blackness, but the fact that he wanted a white child to portray him as a boy in a recently released biographical television movie offers disturbingly strong cir-cumstantial evidence.

6 **Sniping at one another in the workplace,** tattling to the boss about one another and vying for white supervisors' attention and ap-proval, instead of helping one another be better and stronger. This is also fuzzy to detect because competitiveness and "one-upmanship" is part of the white, Western corporate formula for getting ahead, and many African Americans surviving in those settings use the same tactics.

7 **Buying into negative stereotypes about black people's profession-alism and competence.** My grandmother's black neighbor would not be treated by a black doctor or consult a black lawyer because she believed white professionals must be more efficient, better educated and better equipped. This attitude, combined with white racism that assumes black businesses, doctors, and lawyers are for Blacks only, depletes our economic power as well as our unity and pride and self-confidence.

8 **Publicly bashing collective efforts to redress racial wrongs,** such as affirmative action, or criticizing African Americans who are vocal in denouncing racism. The late 1980s ushered in a new, vocal crop of black "conservatives"—mostly men—warmly received by white media and conservative white politicians because they agreed with the white racist notion that, if Blacks aren't "making it," it's only because they

aren't trying hard enough. These people obviously just came to our planet from Oz, and have never heard of racism, injustice, and the canyon that divides black and white economics.

Economist and frequent columnist for *Ms.* magazine, Julianne Malveaux, commenting on the newfound popularity of self-deprecating, so-called conservative African Americans like author Shelby Steele and Supreme Court Justice Clarence Thomas (both naysayers of affirmative action), writes, "While a handful of black male conservatives speak of fair competition and level playing fields, a larger number of African Americans realize that competitions can't be fair when the rules are rigged" (Malveaux, p. 62).

There's probably not much you as a white person can do about manifestations of internalized racism among black people. But it is helpful to recognize them. Rather than blaming the victims for aiding their own oppression, though, we need to understand that systemic racial oppression includes silencing voices of dissent. We need to understand how and why Black-on-Black criticism is rewarded by white social and political institutions and the seats of power in our society. *The Content of Our Character,* Shelby Steele's book maligning affirmative action, got much more mainstream media attention than the myriad of books by black men and women who forthrightly expose racism and espouse affirmative action.

The key for white people truly concerned about overcoming racism is to help create atmospheres of trust and openness, by observing internalized oppression and understanding your role in perpetuating it.

The Hair-Texture-and-Skin-Color Thang

Since slavery, the politics of skin color and hair texture have been controversial and painful issues within the African-American community. Biracial children of black slaves and white slave owners often used their lighter complexions and eyes and straight hair as means of survival, with white masters often assigning lighter-skinned (read "prettier") slaves the "easier" household duties. (Whether or not this was truly "better" or "preferential" treatment remains to be seen. Wasn't a slave in the house as much in bondage as a slave in the field?) Even today a minority of black Americans with lighter complexions pass for White to escape racial oppression and to achieve better economic and social opportunities.

The ever-present intra-family tensions between so-called "light-skinned" and "dark-skinned" or "good-haired" and "nappy-headed" African Americans are skeletons in our closets that we'd rather not rattle before white people. But the pain, anger, and frustration are always with us, and they affect how we deal with you, too. Darker-skinned African Americans often resent and blame their light-skinned brothers and sisters for preferential treatment afforded the latter group by white racists, rather than attacking the *white racism* that sets the standard and makes the White-is-right rules. On the other hand, some black people are "colorstruck," believing the lighter the skin and the straighter the hair (the closer to White, in other words), the more beautiful the person. A color caste system still exists among some black people. A light-skinned girlfriend told me that her mother (who is chocolate brown) discouraged her from marrying a "too-black" man. "Don't bring home any dark-skinned babies," that black mother told her daughter.

When African Americans equate light skin and straight hair with beauty, to the exclusion of dark skin and short, crimped hair, we aid and abet white racism. While ridicule of and aversion to traditional African hair texture and skin tone began with white people, melding a white majority with a black numerical minority in the United States has created a light-makes-right standard of beauty and acceptance, which has been applied by and used against black people and other people of color within our whole society.

In a February 1, 1993, editorial in *Advertising Age,* communications executive J. Clinton Brown observes that white advertisers commonly give preference to light-skinned black women to epitomize the "attractive" African-American female. While Brown affirms the beauty of black women of all shades, he points out that, when it comes to white male ad execs, "if the storyboard calls for a young, sexually appealing African-American woman, the model will look more like Shari

Belafonte than Whoopi Goldberg." Darker-skinned black women more often play "mother figures," he muses rhetorically, adding, "Made any pancakes lately?" (Brown, p. 19.)

This brand of white, American racism is exported from Western culture to other parts of the world. Referring to blonde Brazilian star Xuxa, a 1992 issue of *People* magazine called her blondness a "national treasure," implying that the majority of Brazilians with darker African or indigenous native hair and skin color are *not* treasures. In a 1990 editorial in *El Hispano* newspaper, Maggie Echazabal Hall reported that Latina woman use more hair bleach and skin lighteners than any other racial group in the United States, which, she said, indicates continued self-deprecation based on skin color among Latinas. And a well-traveled friend tells me that fitness centers in Japan that cater to the corporate trade often advertise for workers who are White, blonde and "Western-looking."

Historically, the issue of skin color has eroded unity and healing within the African-American community. Until the Black-is-beautiful rhetoric of the 1960s, at least one nationally prominent African-American sorority had an unwritten policy restricting its membership to lighter-skinned, straight-haired members. Many black women and men today express a preference for lighter-skinned black dating partners, rather than caramel-colored or smoky brown-skinned ones.

Among African-American women especially, hair texture and skin color continue to be hotly debated issues. Many contend that artificially straightened or natural hair is just a matter of style and preference. For most that may be true. But the fact that words like "nappy," "kinky," "good," and "bad" hair are still used in African-American parlance points to a residual effect of white racism abetted by black people; namely that for some, white people's beauty and style are assumed to be best. At the risk of alienating some of my African-American brothers and sisters, our hair *is* political, whether or not we realize it.

This does not mean that to straighten one's hair is to betray one's Blackness. But to do so without understanding the relevant history can be problematic. And those who straighten their hair and berate a "nappy-headed" brother or sister are indulging in self-hatred.

Black mentors in corporate America often advise black protégés to take down their Afrocentric braids and cut off their dreadlocks so as not to offend white colleagues and business associates and, therefore, impede their own ascent up the corporate ladder. Lawsuits by black television newswomen who have been fired or threatened by bosses because of "ethnic" or "militant" hairstyles (usually braids and dreads) still make headlines. The very fact that Afrocentric hairstyles evoke fear and disapproval in white society, and that so many black people prefer long hair and straightened styles for black women especially, makes it clear that some African Americans are still slaves to white America's notion of flaxen-haired beauty—a self-defeating, self-deflating standard for the majority of those with African hair, complexions and physical features.

The recent increase in plastic surgery among black people seeking to reduce dense lips and noses and the seemingly harmless fad of wearing blue or green contact lenses are rooted in the same self-hatred. For all his philanthropy and musical tributes to racial harmony, Michael Jackson's penchant for skin-lightening and plastic surgery says better than any words that he has a problem with his racial identity and sense of self.

Make no mistake—light can be beautiful. Former Miss America Vanessa Williams is a beautiful woman. So are actors Jasmine Guy, Lonette McKee, singer Mariah Carey and the eternally radiant Lena Horne. But ask yourself why white critics and white surveyors of beauty and style rave over these particular African-American women, most times to the exclusion of their darker-skinned sisters? They are no more beautiful than actors Goldberg, Alfre Woodard, Maya Angelou, Oprah Winfrey, opera star Leontyne Price, or former Supreme Mary Wilson. But green eyes, straighter hair, near-white skin and keen, European features give those in the first list a particular legitimacy according to white notions of beauty.

The white-corporate-male standard of beauty, as the only legitimate standard our society recognizes, also contributes to pandemic mental and physical illnesses in our society that infect not only "nonwhite" adherents to that standard, but Whites themselves. Scores of white American women literally maim and kill themselves to get a tan like

George Hamilton, pouty lips like Michelle Pfeiffer, a nipped-and-tucked body like Cher, and a cleft and chiseled face like Michael Jackson. Anorexia and other eating disorders claim the lives of hundreds of women each year.

So what does all this mean to you, a white liberal person, in your quest to overcome racism? None of us can help how our standards of beauty have been shaped by society, but we can help broaden those standards.

- **Acknowledge your racial biases with regard to beauty** and examine how you may bring these biases into your workplace and other interracial settings. In hiring and interviewing, are you more comfortable with light-skinned black people than with darker-skinned ones? Would you hire a competent receptionist or attorney who was a black woman with dreadlocks and corn-rows? Why not?
- **Talk with your children and buy them black and brown dolls as well as white ones, and storybooks with positive black characters.** When commenting on beauty or reading fairy tales, conjure up images of beautiful princesses and handsome princes representing a variety of body types, skin colors and hair textures. They don't all have to be thin, blond, blue-eyed and "fair." Make sure that your child has a variety of images and body types from which to learn—a beautiful woman can be White or Black; light-skinned, like Lena Horne; dark-skinned, like former congresswoman Barbara Jordan; slim and petite, like singer Whitney Houston; or robust, like comedians Marcia Warfield and Rosanne.
- If you attend church or synagogue, **make sure religious books and Sunday school curricula portray Jesus, Moses, Mary, Noah, and other biblical characters as other than European.** In discussing religious figures with your children or your religious studies class, acknowledge that no one knows the exact appearance of religious figures, and many historians point to evidence that Jesus, for example, was a dark-skinned, wooly-haired Jew.

- **Pass up beauty contests, fashion and beauty shows, and beauty-and-fashion magazines that rarely have people of color on the cover** or in major spreads (or that choose only near-white black people as cover models). Instead, choose periodicals with more diverse images of people. Scan *Essence, Ebony Man,* and other African-American magazines to understand the variety of beautiful men and women in the black community. Create a diverse reading environment for children at home by choosing storybooks, comic books, and magazines with racially diverse images. (They are legion—check out the public library, a black bookstore, or a black-owned newsstand).
- **Look for beauty and depth beyond physical features.** Invest in magazines other than those that deal exclusively with "beauty." Read periodicals that celebrate the deeper beauty of the human spirit, that feature people who contribute to society as a whole. *Sports Illustrated* is great for multicultural images and inspirational stories. A great multicultural world news periodical is *Colors,* the global news magazine published by Benetton clothiers.

BLOOM COUNTY

by Berke Breathed

What Your Black Friends Won't Tell You About Your Racism

"I know a place . . . ain't nobody worryin', ain't no smilin' faces, lyin' to the races. C'mon, I'll take you there . . . "

from "I'll Take You There," by songwriter Alvertis Isbell, 1972

It's the little things that can kill any relationship. This truth applies to those of us seeking to bridge gaps of race and culture in our daily encounters. Sometimes racism isn't a matter of name-calling or exclusion alone; it's process. It's going over a black employee's expenses with a fine-toothed comb, while a white colleague's vouchers go unchecked. It's decorating the office Christmas tree with only blond-haired angels. It's asking the black secretary to sing or dance at the office talent show, then ignoring his suggestions on buying a copy machine that could enhance his efficiency. It's suggesting that your social club's trip to historic Savannah include a tour of a former plantation and a reenactment of a Civil War battle, but opting not to visit the city's Black history museum. It's asking me if your friend can touch my cornrowed hair, as if my style is from another planet.

I'm not one for gathering alone with African-American friends to commiserate about "white folks' insensitivity," unless I'm also willing to do offending white people the courtesy of telling them to their faces that they have said or done something I feel is racist. How else are people going to learn what is and isn't racist if the victims of racism won't help out? So much of what goes on is unconsciously imbedded in our psyches. Confrontation and honest disclosure, though distasteful in "polite" society, are vital methods to overcoming white racism and bringing people close together as a human family.

So, it would be unfair for me to write a book like this without giving white liberals some crib notes straight from an informed source on how to fast-check self-propelled white racism.

The following list is woefully incomplete, but it will help you recognize—and curb—your most common expressions of racism and racial ignorance at work and in other interracial settings:

Work Ethics

1 **Unless you have tried to talk it out with (and get no satisfaction from) a black employee with whom you have a problem, don't automatically go to his or her white boss or co-worker for help.** Not only do you deny that African American the opportunity to learn from mistakes, you make her or him seem less competent and trustworthy in the eyes of the powers that be. A friend of mine who was a business writer for a newspaper—and a black woman—was plagued constantly by a white business leader who would call her white male boss to complain about mistakes in her news articles, rather than calling them directly to her attention. Subsequently, she was forced to resign without ever knowing that she had presented budget figures in error. She did, however, earn a reputation for being "unreliable."

2 **Share all the rules—written and unwritten—that will enable African Americans to succeed at your company.** Many of the most important tips for success are not written in a company handbook; rather, they are shared informally among co-workers. If you know the boss hates red nail polish, tell the new black woman as well as the new white woman in your office. If the supervisor gives brownie points to workers who eat at their desks instead of taking a one-hour lunch, let *all* your colleagues in on it.

3 **Think racial inclusiveness when organizing both formal and informal work-related gatherings, no matter how insignificant those**

gatherings may seem. Says Walterene Swanston, director of minority affairs for the ANPA Foundation, "On their first day of work, introduce new minority staffers to other employees, not only other minority employees. Make sure they are part of informal lunch or dinner gatherings." First impressions are lasting, so make sure that African-American newcomers meet as many people as possible along the company's chain of command, especially their supervisors and their supervisors' supervisors. Introduce them to the people in the personnel and benefits office; introduce them to your regular gang during coffee break. That's often where many important company decisions are made and information shared ("Ten tips," p. 12).

4 **If you are just beginning to address racial inclusiveness at work, do not start with token efforts,** like asking African Americans to entertain at office parties; *begin* by putting African-Americans in decision-making positions. I recently attended a meeting where a news photographer wanted a shot of the company's management team. Since the entire team was White and male—and the CEO was concerned about "image"—the men dragged a file clerk, an African-American woman, into the group for the photo session. How insulting. Instead of putting on a false front for the media, the executives' energies would have been better spent recruiting and training African-Americans for manager positions.

A few years ago, because of my musical ability, my agency exec began asking me to sing and lead a recreational "icebreaker" to start a business meeting. I was flattered until I realized that, once the entertainment portion of the meeting was over, the serious responsibilities and important decisions were handed over to my white male colleagues.

If you want to increase visibility for people of color in your company, hire and equip them for leadership at all levels. Then you won't have to strain to appear racially inclusive.

5 Swanston also advises employers to **rethink who goes to professional enhancement and training programs.** "Sending only white staff members could be construed as an attempt not to develop others."

A white executive lobbied for our company to pay a day's travel expenses for white clerical employees who wanted to attend our agency's international convention—just to "look around" and see what the "professional" staff was involved in. The white executive was annoyed when the African-American personnel director suggested issuing an open invitation to all interested clerical workers (a large percentage of whom are people of color) in order to achieve racial balance and provide equal access. The white executive thought the move unnecessary, but the black woman was aware that access to even the smallest enrichment opportunities can open the door to something bigger.

6 If you are a supervisor, **support your black employees' professionalism, right to control their own budgets, to be self-motivating, and do their work without you looking over their shoulders.** To many of our white clients, especially, I'm still the "new" kid in our news office, even after ten years. Several longtime clients still insist upon calling on my white, fifty-ish male boss when "big" decisions have to be made. The first time it happened, my boss acted as the front man and passed the legwork to me. Finally, I insisted—and he agreed—that he back me up by referring people directly to me.

This goes for financial officers, too. Do you scrutinize expense vouchers of certain staff members while letting others breeze through? Line up those names on both lists. Where are the black people's names? Are you being a good financial manager or a racist one?

7 **When planning a staff meeting or other kind of business meeting, allow ample free time for participants to do their own thing.** Don't require everyone to eat together at every meal, or expect everyone to spend free time together. It's nothing personal. Often, black people do not feel totally comfortable letting our hair down in a White-dominated work environment. While the white guy at the office Christmas party might get drunk and dance on the table the night before and land the big account the next day, an African-American employee would never hear the end of any such antics (remember the double standard). It becomes part of the "case" against our competency and professionalism.

So, if you really want to give your employees "down time" during a meeting, allow time for people to be alone, or to eat and socialize in the intimate groups of their choice.

Social Graces

8 **Don't expect us to discuss our personal affairs; don't be nosy.** If you're a friend to an African-American co-worker, and that co-worker wants you to know something personal, she'll tell you. No, this is not just a white problem; but in interracial situations, black people many times get burned when they share seemingly benign information with some white colleagues. We've learned to be selective due to bad experiences. Personal problems, especially, get translated into weaknesses and shortcomings. This is both a result of racism and of the only-the-strong-survive corporate mentality.

For example, I had a hysterectomy a few years ago. White women in my company who had never even spoken to me called my secretary to find out exactly what kind of surgery I was having. There was subsequent speculation about my sexual preferences, "reasons behind" my marital status (I was single at the time), my prospects for ever marrying, and whether or not my "health problems" would be a drain on the agency. Those speculations made the rounds even to our clients in other agencies (which is where I first heard the gossip). And the women who were so anxious to know didn't even send flowers.

9 **Don't *ever* tell racist jokes or make racist comments,** especially in front of African Americans, even if those comments concern other-than-Black ethnic groups. Such comments are racist, and if black people laugh or join in, they too are participating in white racism. Don't talk about "those foreigners," and expect black people to nod assent. If you're spouting racist rhetoric, you're no friend. Most African Americans know that the white person who says "wetback" or "chink" to our faces will say "nigger" behind our backs.

10 Respect our cultural expressions; don't make light of them. A white co-worker—and frequent Friday-night dancing partner—attended my traditional African-American church with me one Sunday. Our choir was rocking to a gospel song, and the congregation was swaying and clapping. He, misunderstanding our historic expression of the sacred, started snapping his fingers and grinding his hips as if he were dancing to James Brown's "Sex Machine." For me, ours was sacred movement; for him, it was a free-for-all. What he should have done is be still and learn.

Amoja Three Rivers tells similar stories about some white people who think it appropriate to act "savage" or "wild" when attending African drumming and dance ceremonies. She advises:

> If you are a white person, and you happen upon people of color drumming and dancing, and you want to join in but you don't know if you should or not, use these unclear occasions as opportunities for meditation and centering.
>
> *It's okay for you not to be the center of everything you see* [emphasis mine]. People of color sometimes need to have the time and space to explore our heritage and traditions . . . This does not necessarily mean that you must go away. It does mean that at such times we usually prefer that white people maintain an outer circle as allies and observers, rather than spontaneous and uninvited participants. It's fine to be patient, be still and just listen.

. . . and don't touch my hair!

Besides the fact that it insults African Americans to be petted like a poodle or stared at like an object in a curiosity shop, it really bugs me that, after four-hundred-plus years of Black-White cohabitation in this country, many white people seem to know so little about our grooming habits and preferences that African Americans practically have to conduct a lesson in African-American beauty culture every time we comb our hair in a bicultural setting.

Being immersed in the "majority" culture, *we* know that some white people bleach their hair. (We, too, can usually tell the difference between a bleached blond and a natural one.) We know some tan their skin. (We just don't know *why*, since opinion polls show that most Whites would not want to become Black). We know that you have to wash your hair much more frequently than we wash ours because your hair generally is more oily.

That's why black people, as a rule, don't often ask to touch white people's newly styled hair or ask naive questions. We see the personal habits of white people played out daily in movies, television commercials, and in books and plays. Since white people's lifestyles are considered the cultural "norm," they are part of popular cultural knowledge, shared even among those of us for whom such knowledge is irrelevant.

So maybe you can understand why we—who have lived in the same country with white Americans for four centuries—are annoyed to find ourselves the continued objects of white curiosity. A couple of summers ago I was hanging out by a pool, soaking up some sun while reading. A college-educated white friend expressed amazement that black people "get darker" in the sun. Darker-skinned white people get faster, deeper tans because they have more pigment to welcome the sun, right? Doesn't it stand to reason that a chocolate brown person, who has even more sun-friendly pigment, can also get a tan?

My cornrowed head cannot get through a cordon of white people at a business meeting or social function without at least three white people wanting to touch it, ask me how long it takes to "do" it, and inquire how long the style will last. My friends with dreadlocks have even more stories. One African-American college professor saw a white mother snatch her child from the professor's path and warn the child that people with "hair like that" are drug addicts. Another time, a white father on the subway asked my friend to let his kid feel her hair.

Any African American who has lived in a dormitory at a predominantly white college has a yarn to tell about the first time white roommates discovered that some of us straighten our hair with a hot comb. At the University of Tennessee in the 1970s, I was my gang's hairdresser. One night, during my freshman year, a white girl called the fire department on us because she thought we were burning our dorm room. Actually, what she smelled was a hot plate, Royal Crown Pomade, and fried African hair.

From that time forward we had a regular, captive audience of white classmates armed with a barrage of questions every time I pressed a head of hair. Had it been an official course I would have earned tenure as a professor.

No matter how "interesting" or "unusual" our hairstyles seem to you, for us they are business as usual. We generally do not like uninvited hands touching our dreadlocks and rubbing our braids. That's just plain rude. For those of you who are curious but fearful of appearing ignorant, here's some inside dope about black folks' hairstyles and how we achieve them:

Naturals or Afros. Black American hair comes in all textures, from tight and curly to bone straight. From our African ancestors comes thick, wooly, naturally crimped hair. Many people with hair this texture wear "naturals" (sometimes called "Afros" or " 'fros"). Generally, the only maintenance for a natural is keeping it cut, cleaned, conditioned, and moisturized. (Unlike white folks' hair, which has to be washed often during the week because of oil and dirt buildup, drier, fragile African hair requires gentle handling and shampooing, usually no more than once a week.) For daily care we also use moisturizers—known in old-fashioned parlance as "hair grease," although modern versions are lightweight oils, mousses, or creams.

Perming, Pressing, Straightening. Although European ancestry has given some African Americans straight hair, the majority of black people who seem to have "like-White" straight hair achieve this look artificially. This can be done by chemicals (called a "permanent," "perm," or "relaxer"), or by "pressing" clean, dried hair with a heated metal comb. Relaxers last from four to six weeks, until the naturally textured hair grows out about one-half inch from the roots. Then a "touch-up" is required. Heat-pressed hair lasts until the next washing (weekly is best), when it will "go back" to its natural crimped texture. It then must be pressed again.

Braids and Cornrows. It can take anywhere from two to twenty-four hours to cornrow or braid our hair, depending on how elaborate the style and how adept the stylist. Technically speaking, cornrows are plaited close to the scalp; braids hang loose. The style can last up to four months. Yes, you can wash it without taking the braids apart. Yes, the hair grows while braided. (Incidentally, although this style is also popular with some white people, it is erroneous and insulting to call it the "Bo Derek look" in honor of the white actor who wore braids in the 1979 movie 10. Braids and cornrows have been worn by African and Afro-Caribbean women for centuries. African-American actor Cicely Tyson popularized the U.S. version in the 1970s. See the preceding chapter.)

That wet, curly look (Jheri or California curls). The look (à la Michael Jackson) is achieved by a chemical process (similar to "perming"). Called "Jheri curls" or "California curls," the hair is chemically treated, twisted onto rods, and dried.

Once the process is completed, moisturizing is the key, and people sleep in plastic caps (like shower caps) to keep the hair moist and pillows unsullied. Despite its wet look, the process dries the hair terribly; thus the moisturizing lotions are applied daily. Most amateurs overdo it, which is why some look drippy and messy. You may remember the hilarious stained couch scene from Eddie Murphy's 1988 movie *Coming to America.*

Weaves. Many people of all races—especially in the entertainment industry—add length and volume to their hair by having false hair "woven in." A "good" weave is nearly impossible to detect. Natural hair is braided or bound, and false hair (human or synthetic) is woven, glued, or sewn in. Weaves enhance braided and cornrowed hair, or add height and volume to straightened hair.

Dreadlocks. Dreadlocks—currently worn by actors Whoopi Goldberg and Joie Lee, activist-educator Angela Davis and author Alice Walker—are considered antennae to the "Jah," or the Creator, by some Afro-

Caribbean religious believers called Rastafarians. Not all people who wear dreads are Rastafarians, however. Dreadlocked hair is, in fact, locked hair, a natural bonding process for African hair. As it grows the hair can be twisted by hand to create smooth, even locks. It is not easily combed out; usually, to change styles, the hair must be cut off, allowed to grow and then restyled. Most who wear dreadlocks maintain them by keeping them scrupulously clean (yes, you can wash them), moisturizing the scalp, and re-twisting loosening locks (some use beeswax or a waxy pomade to secure).

Your Rights as a Sincere, Recovering Racist

"...and the trouble is, if you don't risk anything, you risk even more..."

Erica Jong, author

My husband insists that he's "helping" me when he washes dishes or takes out the garbage, even though we both live in the house, both eat and manufacture garbage, and both work forty-plus hours a week. Larry's good about doing his share, mind you, but he wants ample praise for it. But when I come home nightly and I cook, he never thanks *me*. He usually just complains that there's not enough salt in the turnip greens.

Likewise, many white liberals are looking for praise for being liberal and at least trying. Racism is an ugly word and, after all, compared to Pat Buchanan and Rush Limbaugh, you're probably light-years ahead. (The fact that you're even reading this book points to that.) So, you're tired of carrying the harsh weight of being called "white racist."

But, as I said at the beginning, if you think *you're* tired of being called racist, think how weary *we* are of dealing with it. And, in terms of the lasting effects on black people's lives, a "well-meaning" white co-worker who tells an off-color joke or a "really nice" white boss who again passes us over for a deserved promotion is as hurtful as the sheet-wearing terrorist who burns a cross on the lawn. And the effects of the former expressions can often have more dire implications for us.

If you're sincerely making an effort to understand the holistic nature of white racism and endeavoring to root it out, starting with yourself,

then you understand there's a lot more to be done before we hand out
wholesale Nobel Prizes.

Still, as a human being and a recovering racist who is truly trying,
you are justified in expecting some understanding and consideration
from African Americans and other people of color. Namely, you have
the right to:

1 Not feel guilty when you inadvertently do or say something racist.
In fact, your guilt-tripping isn't helping anyone—certainly not us.
Sincere white people and sincere black people have a common goal: to
clear the air, and understand and relate to one another better.
Unfortunately, being born White in the U. S. has contributed racism to
your frame of reference. But don't feel guilty—feel compelled to
change.

2 Not be accused of racism when racism is clearly not in play. Several years ago, a black woman—since fired from our company—
stole money from several co-workers' purses (including two black
women and a white woman). When the white colleague caught her
and reported her, the thief called the white woman a "racist." That may
or may not have been true, but the white woman was *not* showing
racist behavior by defending her own property, and "Sister-girl" had no
business in anyone else's purse.

3 Make mistakes as you grow. You shouldn't be afraid to say or do
anything—the goal is for you to uncover and correct your racist
patterns, not merely to hide them. It's okay to make mistakes, if you
are sincere about wanting to do better. White liberals *should,* however,
know better than to use racial slurs, tell racist jokes, and some of that
overt stuff.

4 Take a hard line with an African-American person who deserves
a hard line. An incompetent employee needs to be reprimanded
or fired; a person who commits a crime should be punished; a colleague who is disloyal can be called on the carpet—regardless of race.

Just think twice before you act and look in the mirror. Are punishments and reprimands meted out equitably? Are you reacting *exactly* as you would with another white person? Or is racism coloring your perspective?

5 Be angry or annoyed when confronted about your racism. No one likes to be called down for his or her behavior or language, especially when one thinks of oneself as progressive. But be open to criticism, even while the manner in which you are criticized may bug you. You may learn something, and, instead of pretending to be open, the next time you really will be.

6 Disagree with someone's assessment of your behavior or speech as "racist." There are always two sides to every story. Just remember that it usually costs a person of color a great deal to raise the issue of racism, even if the cost is a lower comfort level at the mostly white office or club. Think twice about what she or he is saying to you about racism. Check with another African-American colleague or white liberal friend for their opinions. Reexamine your own behavior. After serious self-examination and feedback from others, if you truly disagree with that person, say so. And at least be sensitive to his or her individual concern.

7 Ask questions on unclear issues of white racism and race relations. Be aware, however, that black people have the right to be suspicious or annoyed about your asking. We sometimes grow weary of teaching racial etiquette. Ask yourself if you're asking questions for clarification or understanding or as a way to stonewall and avoid dealing with your own racial blind spots. If your motives are pure, choose a private space and a person of color you trust—and who trusts you— and ask your questions. Then listen. If your relationship with this black person is strong and honest, you'll ask the right questions, and that person will take it in the right spirit and give you some useful feedback.

8 Maintain relationships with white friends and relatives who are not racially "aware" and "progressive". Your loved ones are your loved ones. But it's trickier than you think to grow from being racist yourself when "significant others" are racist. You don't have to preach, but you should never, ever participate in racist activities or conversation. If it is too awkward and uncomfortable to confront your Uncle Bill while he regales the family with racist jokes, at least be silent and don't laugh. Later, when you're alone, you might say, "Uncle Bill, that joke made me feel kind of funny. I have a friend, Josh, and he's Black and he's not like that at all." Or you might make a point of ushering small children out of the room when the off-color stuff starts. If anyone asks later, simply say, "We're trying to teach the children to respect everyone and not use those kinds of words." Be as incensed as you would be if Uncle Bill had masturbated in front of you and your children. Racism is a social disease—stop it from spreading.

Making Your Home and Your Head (and Your Children) Racism-Free

"Beloved, we are all God's children now;
what we will be has not yet been revealed."
I John 3:2, New Revised Standard Version of the Bible, 1989

"You are a child of the universe, no less than the trees and the stars;
you have a right to be here. And whether or not it is clear to you, no
doubt the universe is unfolding as it should."
from the poem "Desiderata" by Max Ehrmann, 1927

Each preceding chapter offers some suggestions for monitoring and eliminating verbal expressions and gestures of white racism in some of its most common manifestations. However, your personal habits (and those of your family) and the environment at home, in the office, in social settings, and the political arena can also be modified to thwart white racism. The following are specific first steps for creating a racism-free space wherever you are. You're probably already doing many of these, but try expanding your efforts.

At home

1 **Create a multiracial, multimedia environment for everyday use, not just for show.** It's not enough to have posters and artifacts from the annual African-American street fair. Derman-Sparks says at least half the images encountered by white children should include people of color "in order to counter the White-centered images of the dominant culture" (Derman-Sparks, p. 13).

Buy your children black dolls as well as white ones, and read to them from books by black authors with multiracial illustrations. Begin in their infancy—studies show that racist behavior is learned from as early as age two. Let children watch *The Wiz* with Diana Ross as well as *The Wizard of Oz* with Judy Garland—both have merit. For the adults in the house, let your video, compact disc, and print libraries reflect multiculturalism.

And educate yourselves. Some titles every home should consider are: "Eyes on the Prize," a PBS television series on the Civil Rights movement; "Roots," the television series based on the Alex Haley saga; recorded speeches by Martin Luther King, Jr., Malcolm X, Sojourner Truth, etc.; the book *Roots* by Alex Haley and any of a number of Black history books.

2 Read "black" magazines and newspapers—they're for everyone. *Newsweek* isn't considered a "white" magazine, although the majority of stories and pictures are about white people. Magazines written from a black perspective or geared to a primarily black audience were developed to provide us a forum—we've long been excluded from others. But you can read them, too. *Essence, Black Collegiate,* and *Ebony* will offer you another perspective.

3 Ban racist language in the house, just as you would pornographic or profane language. Don't you say it in front of the children and discipline them if they say it. If you won't let them call grandma "bitch," don't let them call African Americans "nigger." Set limits—maligning a person because of race and ethnicity should not be tolerated. Elicit from your children any negative racial feelings, and help them understand the difference between problems they might have with an individual and sweeping generalizations about whole racial groups. Explain clearly what words and actions hurt others—don't just say, "That's not nice." Do not allow racist language from visiting adults—act as you would if they proposed to defecate on your living room floor. Protect your children's minds.

4 Monitor television shows and movies for racist overtones and undertones. Encourage your children to watch programs and movies that portray African Americans in a positive light—they'll get *plenty* of negative stuff from other media outside your control. From "Sesame

Street" to "In the Heat of the Night," make sure positive role models and heroes are other than European Americans. Until children are old enough to make decisions about their viewing habits, do not let them watch shows with overwhelmingly negative images of African Americans. (Are the black characters portrayed only as criminals, welfare recipients, homeless people, or clowns?) If you must watch these shows as a family, discuss them with your kids and help them separate fact from racist fiction.

5 Socialize with African Americans and other people of color. This is tricky, because you don't want to recruit friends *solely* on the basis of race, then flaunt them as proof of your liberalness. Nothing is as effective as interaction with people, however, so stretch yourself. Invite an African-American co-worker to lunch, to happy hour after work, to bring his kids along with you and your kids to the Christmas parade or the county fair. If you're lucky you'll make a new friend, and nothing beats that. Also, your children will grow up assuming that interracial friendships are possible and acceptable.

6 When possible, patronize Black-owned businesses, physicians, lawyers, etc. Ask friends for recommendations or consult the local NAACP or Urban League for a directory of services and businesses owned and operated by black people. Black businesses aren't just for black people. Not only will you help bolster black economic power and self-determination, but may overcome some prejudices you may have about the quality of black professionalism or trading in a certain part of town.

7 When house hunting, consider a racially mixed neighborhood. At the end of each day, when I drive up to my mailbox, I see a white boy and a black boy peddling their bicycles side by side down my street. At age ten or so, they've been playing together for at least five years. It's no big deal to them, and that's exactly the point. Racism and racial separation are learned; friendship and establishing common ground with those around you is natural.

At your children's schools

1 Survey textbooks, workbooks, and reading lists each term. Make sure that works by African-American authors are on the required reading lists in literature courses, that African-American history is dealt with fully as part of *American* history (and not just slavery and George Washington Carver) in books and audiovisual materials. If a teacher is negligent in those areas, have a conference with that teacher, meet with other parents, make suggestions to the school's PTA chairperson, visit your representatives on the local school board. Make sure that children have access to materials by and about African Americans and other people of color. In meeting with your children's principals and teachers (something every parent should do as a matter of course), be clear that you expect the curriculum to be racially diverse and multicultural. This directive can be especially effective coming from white parents, because it lets educators know that concern for racial inclusiveness is *everybody's* issue.

2 Make sure schools observe Martin Luther King, Jr.'s birthday, African-American History Month, and other celebrations of the contributions and histories of all people of color. Volunteer to help a teacher put up a bulletin board or suggest an assembly speaker from African-American churches and civic organizations.

3 Monitor field trips for racial overtones. When I was in high school a white teacher made us read *Gone With the Wind*—like my pal, Sally, it was her favorite book—and took us to see the movie. While Teacher thrilled over the love story and the antebellum splendor, white students laughed at the arm-waving squealing of Prissy and Mammy. The teacher never related the story to subjugation of black people, never confronted the racism at work in our group. We never read books or stories by other than white authors, and certainly never took a field trip to see movie classics from other-than-White cultures.

4 Push for African-American teachers and students at all levels. If black children are noticeably underrepresented in school-sponsored theater and music programs (and overrepresented on the basketball team), ask why. Often African-American children are not encouraged to develop extracurricular interests other than sports, where Blacks are too often over-represented. If those teachers winning awards from the PTA meetings and at school assemblies are inevitably White, question the criteria and suggest ways to make the processes more inclusive. If your child has African-American teachers, support them whenever you can. If a teacher makes a mistake or does something you don't like, meet and talk with that teacher first, instead of complaining to the principal. If problems continue, that teacher may, of course, need to be disciplined. (Incompetency is color-blind.) However, make sure that you give adequate support to all your children's teachers, regardless of race.

5 Get to know your children's friends and monitor their comments and actions regarding members of other racial groups. If your child makes friends across racial lines, encourage healthy friendships and get to know the parents of their friends. Parents' perspectives on their children's common classes, schools, or daycare centers can help you monitor and work together for better racial inclusiveness. Talk to your children and their friends about racial issues and racism, and monitor your children's behavior and language. Children often mimic their friends, and if your children have racist friends, you may be able to help all of them arrest racist behavior. While it may not always be necessary to discourage friendships with children who espouse racism, help your children develop a strong sense of justice and fairness that will lead them to correct their friends or choose friends who value respect for all people. And, if the opportunity arises, talk to parents of the offending children about their child's racist words and behavior. The parents may not know, and a word from you can help.

At work

1 Push for regularly scheduled anti-racism workshops, and solicit highly visible support for them from the top managers in your company. If the boss seems enthusiastic about it and feels that it's necessary, the other managers will follow suit. For large companies, provide anti-racism training by departments and separately for managers. Include advocacy for people of color in the job description of a designated top-level manager. Advocate for an informal process whereby employees can discuss grievances freely, without fear of reprisals.

2 Support the existence of affinity groups for African Americans and other people of color. In a racist environment, people of color often turn to one another for networking and support. They do not want to exclude you, only to include themselves. If you're really interested in building bridges, suggest to the coordinator of the affinity group that some interracial social or discussion times be scheduled.

3 Confront and/or report any racist actions, harassment, or language to the proper agency authorities, even if you must do it anonymously. Don't let people of color be the only ones to expose and attack white racism. As a white person you may have even more influence with the perpetrator. If possible, in lieu of reporting her or him, take the offending co-worker aside and say a personal word. ("Jim, I don't think your comment about Rosalyn was fair or appropriate. She's a fine employee and it bothered me that you would make a racial slur about her.") If the offense is serious enough (threats, lies, physical harassment), report it to the affirmative action officer or to your supervisor (or to a higher-up whom you can trust). Let the injured party know you're in his or her corner.

4 When contracting work with other companies, make sure you consider and seek out "minority-owned" firms. And not just the cleaning crews or the caterers. Consider African-American attorneys, architects, printers, psychologists. Several years ago a white supervisor sent every African-American employee who complained about racism on the job to a therapist to help them "cope" with their "misconceptions." None of the psychologists on retainer with our company at that time were African American. The situation was rectified, and a few white employees have been to the couch to deal with their racism.

In Social Settings

1 If the membership of your social club, sorority, or fraternity is all White, find out why. Yes, maybe it just happens to be that way. But many times racial exclusion is a long-standing, unspoken policy. If it is policy—either written or unwritten but practiced—challenge it at the highest level. Or, consider the activities and literature of your club. Remember the white sorority and the antebellum ball? People can be made to feel unwelcome without a word being said. If leadership seems amenable to change, open the membership, and work actively to recruit and empower people of color. If leadership and other members do not seem amenable to change, you have a decision to make: work actively for change, go along with the status quo, or quit the club.

2 If your club, your sorority, your church, your plumbers' association, are open to people of color, make sure they also hold positions of leadership, are invited as guest speakers, and used as experts. They shouldn't just take up space and fill token positions .

3 Make sure your house of worship, civic clubs, etc., observe Martin Luther King, Jr.'s birthday, African-American History Month, Women's History Month, etc. Establish a sister relationship with an African-American church or group, and plan joint celebrations around these and other occasions. If your organization is predominantly White, push for multicultural events in order to expose your members to other racial and cultural groups. International dinners, book and craft fairs are excellent events to showcase diversity.

At the Polls—From School Board to U. S. President

1 Let a political candidate's stand on racial issues influence your voting. While none of us can afford to be a one-issue voter, positions on racial issues must be seen as a major factor. Former President George Bush set race relations back seventy-five years and made race-baiting fashionable again with his 1988 Willie Horton-is-the-Black-bogeyman ad campaign. Do *not* vote for candidates who use racist rhetoric, who pit "us" against "them," and who do not have credible people of color as advisors and decision-makers in their campaigns.

2 Look for the subliminal racist messages in campaign rhetoric. Are we really talking about "family" or "traditional" values or do we mean white American values and the nuclear, white family? Are we really trying to reform the social welfare system, or are we taking a swipe at low-income families, single parents, and people of color and blaming oppressed people for their oppression? Is employment improving across the board, or is the gap between white and black family income and employment ignored? Is "law and order" reform a license to harass African-American and Latino males on the street or in their homes, or are we talking about hiring more people of color as police officers and organizing community watch programs? Is your city's redistricting plan addressing legitimate population concerns, or is it an attempt to diffuse black voting power by breaking up large populations of African Americans?

3 Read between the statistical lines and consider the source when reading some surveys and polls. Yes, a disproportionate number of African Americans are in jails and prisons. But the majority are not. And ask yourself why there are so many people of color in the penal system. Why do many white people serve shorter sentences than black people who commit similar offenses? Study the number of black men facing the death penalty compared to white people who commit similar crimes. Lobby for a fair justice system; sign petitions or write a letter to your state legislature.

4 Push for multiracial education in your school system and for multiracial representation on the school board and among faculties in all schools, public or private. It doesn't matter if there are few people of color in the schools. Black history, in fact, is *American* history. African-American History Month should be observed throughout the city and county. History books and social studies books should reflect a multicultural reality. Eurocentric textbooks should be replaced or at least augmented by additional assigned texts and assemblies with knowledgeable guest speakers who are people of color. Get involved in your local PTA, even if you're not a parent. Make sure your tax dollars support balanced, equitable education.

5 Respect boycotts against products and stores reported to discriminate. Before choosing a bank, find out about its investment policies. Is there a commitment to hiring and empowering people of color above the clerical level? I was shopping recently in New Mexico stores that specialized in Native American artifacts, and not one Native American owned or was employed by the shops. This was in a city where sixty percent of the citizens are Navajo. I wouldn't buy from them—I solicited from Native vendors on the streets. A mail-order company I used to buy from started advertising black "mammy" dolls, à la *Gone With The Wind.* I sent a hot letter, cancelled my subscription, and notified the NAACP in the city where the company is based.

It's not just a black problem. Economic power rules the planet, and it *does* make a difference where you spend your money. I was shopping with a white friend recently and we came to a department store being boycotted by black organizations for discrimination in hiring practices. As we approached, my friend said, "Oh, we can't go in here. Let's go somewhere else." Other white people were streaming in the door, but she recognized the discrimination issue as one *she* should reckon with.

6 Vote. It's an old saying, but if you're not part of the solution, you're part of the problem.

Inside Your Head

Believe in the power of good over the evils of racism, and believe that your one altered life can make a big difference. Get it in your mind that every little bit really does help. Make your vote, your dollars, your words, and your actions all count in the war on racism. Every step you take moves us closer to the day when racist walls will come tumbling down, so keep on plugging. We *shall* overcome someday.

Bibliography

"Absence of Blacks in Ads Costs Developer." *The New York Times,* May 16, 1992.

"Afrocentrism in the classroom." *Newsweek,* Sept. 23, 1991.

Agne, Joseph Edward. "Wounded, the Beast Still Exists." *Christian Social Action,* July–Aug. 1992, 4–8. Washington: United Methodist General Board of Church and Society.

Applebome, Peter. "Sons of the South: A new breed." *The Tennessean,* Nov. 15, 1992, sec. D, 1, 3.

Barndt, Joseph. *Dismantling Racism: The Continuing Challenge to White America.* Minneapolis: Augsburg Fortress Press, 1991.

"Beyond Black & White: Rethinking Race and Crime in America." Cover articles in *Newsweek,* May 18, 1992.

"Black Americans reclaim their history." *Newsweek,* Sept. 23, 1991.

"Black/Asian Conflict: Where do we begin?" *Ms.,* Nov.–Dec. 1991, 63.

"Black or White." *Newsweek,* Dec. 30, 1991.

"Blacks and police: up against a wall." *Newsweek,* May 11, 1992.

"Black youth less likely to use drugs, alcohol than whites: Sullivan says." *Jet,* June 1, 1992.

Brown, J. Clinton. "Which black is beautiful?" *Advertising Age,* Feb. 1, 1993, 19.

Burton, M. Garlinda. "Working toward racial/ethnic inclusion: an over-view." From *A Handbook for Conference Directors of Communications,* ed. by Daniel Gangler. Nashville: United Methodist Communications, 1989, 45–48.

"Boycott by blacks costs Miami." *Chicago Tribune,* Jan. 27, 1991, 21.

Childress, Alice. *Like One of the Family: Conversations from a Domestic's Life.* Boston: Beacon Press, 1986.

Contreras, Raoul Lowery. "Welfare Cases We Don't Read About in the White Press." *El Hispano,* July 22, 1992.

Daniels, George M. "A Continuation of Injustice." In *engage/social action forum,* October 1981, 29–32. Washington: United Methodist General Board of Church and Society.

Derman-Sparks, Louise, and the A. B. C. Task Force. *Anti-Bias Curriculum: Tools for Empowering Young Children.* Washington: National Association for the Education of Young Children, 1989.

Gregory, Deborah. "Hair-Raising Tales." *Essence,* Jan. 1992, 56.

Guidelines for Selecting Bias-Free Textbooks and Storybooks. New York: Council on Interracial Books for Children, 1980.

Hall, Maggie Echazabal. "Latinas Don't Need to Be Blond, Blue-Eyed." *El Hispano,* April 1990.

Haywood, Gar Anthony. "Advice for well-meaning whites." *Los Angeles Times.*

Jamison, Charles N., Jr. "Racism: The Hurt that Men Won't Name." *Essence,* Nov. 1992, 64.

Joseph, Gloria I., and Jill Lewis. *Common Differences: Conflicts in Black and White Feminist Perspectives.* Boston: South End Press, 1981.

Karimakwenda, Tererai T. "Beauty and the Beholder." *Essence,* Sept. 1992, 40.

Katz, Judy H. *White Awareness: Handbook for Anti-Racism Training.* Norman, Okla.: University of Oklahoma Press, 1989.

Ledbetter, James. "Imitation of Life." *Vibe,* fall 1992.

Maggio, Rosalie. *The Nonsexist Word Finder: A Dictionary of Gender-Free Usage.* Boston: Beacon Press, 1988.

Malveaux, Julianne. "What you said about race." *Ms.,* May–June 1992, 24–30.

Malveaux, Julianne. "Why Are the Black Conservatives All Men?" *Ms.,* March–Apr. 1991, 61–62.

McCormick, John and Vern E. Smith. " 'Can We Get Along?' " *Newsweek,* Nov. 9, 1992, 70.

Morgan, Robin. "Whose Free Press Is It, Anyway?" *Ms.,* July–Aug. 1991, 1.

Morris, Calvin. "We the [White] People: A History of Oppression." *Sojourners,* Nov. 1987, p. 1821.

Morse, Libby. "Walls of Prejudice." *Chicago Tribune,* Sec. 7, 13–14.

Njeri, Itabari. "Who is black?" *Essence,* Vol. 22, No. 5, 64.

Norment, Lynne. "Who's black and who's not?" *Ebony,* March 1990, 134–138.

Page, Clarence. "Black crime and the chasm between 'correct' and 'right.' " *Chicago Tribune,* Jan. 9, 1991.

Quindlen, Anna. "Affirmative action and the great white myth." *Chicago Tribune,* Jan. 21, 1992.

"Race: our dilemma still." *Newsweek,* May 11, 1992.

"Racism in News," pamphlet and video written by Sharon Maeda. Nashville: Media Action Research Center, Inc., 1991.

Raitt, Bonnie, as quoted in "Words of the Week." *Jet,* Dec. 14, 1992, 32.

Raybon, Patricia. "A case of 'severe bias.' " *Newsweek,* Oct. 2, 1989, 11.

Strickland, William. "Whose History Is It, Anyway?" *Essence,* April 1992, 130.

"Ten tips for managing diversity." From *ASNE Multicultural Management Guide,* March 1992, 12.

Three Rivers, Amoja. *Cultural Etiquette: A Guide for the Well-Intentioned.* Indian Valley, Va.: Market Wimmin, 1990.

Wellman, David T. *Portraits of White Racism.* New York: Cambridge University Press, 1977.

"What to call people of color." *Newsweek,* Feb. 27, 1989.